"I don' **care a**

"Yeah, just not enough to do something about it."

With that, Rafe drew back, taking his heat and charged energy with him. "I'll admit you gave me a good shock Friday night. But you know I'll take care of the baby—medical bills, daycare— whatever you need."

Feeling a bit of pity that he could see no joy, nor feel any hope, at the miracle they'd created together, she reached up and brushed her fingertips across his smooth, warm jaw. His pulse leaped beneath her touch and she smiled sadly. "My brave, noble, do-the-right-thing Rafe. That's the big issue, isn't it? I don't think you understand what I really need." She pulled her hand down to her distended belly. "What *we* really need. And if you do, I don't know if you'll ever be able to give it."

"I don't want you to get hurt, Josie, I care about you."

JULIE MILLER

PROTECTING THE PREGNANT WITNESS

Harlequin®

TORONTO NEW YORK LONDON
AMSTERDAM PARIS SYDNEY HAMBURG
STOCKHOLM ATHENS TOKYO MILAN MADRID
PRAGUE WARSAW BUDAPEST AUCKLAND

In memory of George M. Binger, Jr.
1930-2010
My first hero.
My dad.

Recycling programs
for this product may
not exist in your area.

ISBN-13: 978-0-373-69563-8

PROTECTING THE PREGNANT WITNESS

ABOUT THE AUTHOR

Julie Miller attributes her passion for writing romance to all those fairy tales she read growing up, and to shyness. Encouragement from her family to write down all those feelings she couldn't express became a love for the written word. She gets continued support from her fellow members of the Prairieland Romance Writers, where she serves as the resident "grammar goddess." This award-winning author and teacher has published several paranormal romances. Inspired by the likes of Agatha Christie and Encyclopedia Brown, Ms. Miller believes the only thing better than a good mystery is a good romance.

Born and raised in Missouri, she now lives in Nebraska with her husband, son and smiling guard dog, Maxie. Write to Julie at P.O. Box 5162, Grand Island, NE 68802-5162.

Books by Julie Miller

HARLEQUIN INTRIGUE

841—POLICE BUSINESS*
880—FORBIDDEN CAPTOR
898—SEARCH AND SEIZURE*
947—BABY JANE DOE*
966—BEAST IN THE TOWER
1009—UP AGAINST THE WALL**
1015—NINE-MONTH PROTECTOR**
1070—PROTECTIVE INSTINCTS‡
1073—ARMED AND DEVASTATING‡
1090—PRIVATE S.W.A.T. TAKEOVER‡
1099—KANSAS CITY CHRISTMAS‡
1138—PULLING THE TRIGGER
1176—BEAUTY AND THE BADGE‡
1201—TAKEDOWN*
1245—MAN WITH THE MUSCLE
1266—PROTECTING PLAIN JANE†
1296—PROTECTING THE PREGNANT WITNESS†

* The Precinct
**The Precinct: Vice Squad
‡The Precinct: Brotherhood of the Badge
†The Precinct: SWAT

CAST OF CHARACTERS

Sergeant Rafe Delgado—Point man and second in command of KCPD's premier SWAT Team 1. Self-appointed protector to his slain partner's daughter. After a botched mission, he turned to a friend and comfort flared into passion for one brief night. Now he's worried that he may be the danger she needs protecting from the most.

Josie Nichols—Nursing student. Bartender. Six months' pregnant and the only surviving witness who can identify a serial killer. As the murderer closes in, determined to silence her, she turns to her former best friend Rafe to protect her—and the baby he doesn't yet know is his.

Robbie Nichols—Josie's uncle. Owner of the Shamrock Bar.

Patrick Nichols—Josie's half brother.

Detective Spencer Montgomery—The KCPD detective investigating the Rich Girl Killer murders.

Jake Lonergan—New bartender at the Shamrock Bar.

Steve Lassen—A reporter with a nose for news? Or an annoying thorn in SWAT Team 1's backside?

Jeffrey Beecher—The event planner putting together KCPD's summer carnival to raise money for the widows and orphans fund.

Bud Preston—This perennial lowlife and odd-job man keeps showing up in the most unexpected places.

The Rich Girl Killer—Who is he?

Prologue

The Past

It was a bone-deep instinct to shut down his emotions and simply survive that allowed Rafe Delgado to tune out the world and squeeze the trigger.

Aaron was down. The car had plowed right through him, tossing him into the air and speeding past as he landed with an ominous thud on the pavement of the busy Kansas City street.

Bang.

And then the world rushed in and the fear welled up as snapshot images and jarring noises etched themselves indelibly on his battered soul. Shouts. Curses. Lights flashing. Sirens wailing. Radio static. Screams. The squealing, grating crunch of a car spinning on its blown-out tire and slamming into the bricks of a building down the block from the bank the driver and passengers had just robbed.

"Aaron?" No. Hell no. Rafe holstered his weapon and ran. He put out one hand to stop a truck turning the corner in front of him and radioed in the call for an ambulance. They'd been the first cops on the scene to answer the bank's silent alarm. Rafe's partner—veteran cop, friend, mentor—had said they needed to stop the getaway car. It was harder to catch a gang of thieves once they were on the run than to stop them before they escaped. They'd stopped them, all right. "Aaron!"

This wasn't happening. It couldn't be happening. Rafe Delgado was finally making something of himself. Learning to be a cop, learning to trust. Learning from the best. Sergeant Aaron Nichols was a friend and father, his confessor, as much as he was his partner. The perps had ignored Aaron's warning, had ignored his gun. Rafe had stopped them, but not soon enough.

Barely aware of the other uniformed cops swarming the neighborhood—stopping traffic, herding bystanders off the street, pulling the three dazed and injured criminals out of the car and handcuffing them on the sidewalk—Rafe ran to his fallen partner where he lay bent and broken in the middle of the intersection. Ignoring the pool of blood staining his knees, he knelt down beside Aaron.

"Aaron?" Those deep blue eyes, set between lines of laughter and wisdom, struggled to focus. Rafe scooped up his partner's beefy hand and squeezed it, drawing Aaron's attention. "I got ya, Sarge. Hang in there. The ambulance is on its way."

Aaron's scarred-up boxer's paw tightened weakly around Rafe's fingers. A breathy hint of his Americanized brogue whispered, "Did we get 'em?"

"I shot the tire and they spun out. Save your energy. Don't talk." His hand was cold. There was too much blood. Rafe lifted his head and shouted wildly. "Medic! I need a medic!"

The thick fingers convulsed around Rafe's. "This one's bad, sonny. No doctor can help me."

"That's Irish bull. You stop bleedin'. You hear me?"

Aaron's pale, trembling lips curved in a familiar grin. "Givin' me orders. Who outranks who?"

"Just trying to keep you around, old man." He wanted to apply pressure to the wound bleeding so profusely at the back of his head. But that meant rolling him over, and Rafe was certain from each shallow wheeze for breath that there were internal injuries and that moving him could make things worse. Rafe's eyes filled with tears and he swiped away the useless evidence of emotion to keep his partner's face in focus. "Aaron, tell me what to do."

Aaron's eyes grew distant. He knew he was dying. He knew. "You're a good cop. I knew you would be. I'm proud of you, son."

The faint trill of his native Irish accent was evident even with each gasp. He'd brought his son to this country when his first wife had died. His second wife had given him a daughter and divorced him. He was the best KCPD had to offer. He'd been through too much. He didn't deserve to die like this.

Fluid gurgled in Aaron's throat. "Rafe?"

"I'm right here. What do you need?"

He summoned his strength and squeezed Rafe's hand one last time. "You take care of my Josie. Patrick, too. This'll be hard on them. They need someone to depend on."

Rafe nodded. "I'll be the big brother they never had. Until you get better."

"You'll…need family, too."

"You're my family. Now shut up. Save your strength."

"Got to say this… A father worries…" Rafe wouldn't know. The man who'd sired him hadn't worried about anything but his booze and keeping child services out of his hair. Years of practice shut down the memories of pain and anger and betrayal that tried to rear their ugly head. Aaron needed him. His bloody fingers were scratching blindly across his belt. "Where's my badge?"

"Here." Rafe plucked the scuffed-up badge off the pavement and put it into his hand before pulling them both onto Aaron's chest. "Your badge is right with you, Sarge. Feel it?" The blue eyes drifted shut. "Sarge! Stay with me!"

They opened again. "Take care of my girl. Such a good heart. She has…crush…on you."

"I know. With you watching over my shoulder, nothing will ever happen."

"No, I…damn." A shallow rale stuttered through his chest.

"Aaron?"

"Watch Patrick…he'll fight ya."

"I can handle him."

His eyes opened and closed in lieu of a nod. "I love them. Tell 'em that."

"I will."

"You're…better man…than you think."

The tears chafed beneath his eyelids. "Quit talking like you're—"

"Promise me…protect them."

And then Aaron's scrappy boxer's fist went slack. His eyes glazed over and he was gone.

"I promise."

Chapter One

Rafael Delgado wore jeans, a badge and black leather well.

As he uncrossed his long legs and pulled away from the black heavy-duty pickup he'd been leaning against in the nearly deserted parking lot behind Kansas City's Shamrock Bar, Josie Nichols got a glimpse of the gun he wore on his belt, too. She smiled, unafraid, her pulse doing its customary flutter at the broad shoulders and fluid stride of the man who'd waited in the dark to walk her to her car nearly every night since she'd taken the job tending bar at her uncle's tavern four years earlier.

But then Rafe had been looking out for her almost ten years now, ever since he'd made a promise to her father—his first partner at KCPD—on the night Aaron Nichols had died.

Josie locked the Shamrock's back door and shook off the sadness that tightened her shoulders at the memory of her father's senseless slaughter in the line of duty. She could hear the assurance of booted footsteps crunching on the asphalt behind her. The shadows wouldn't be so scary tonight. The loneliness she lived with wouldn't prick so sharply. Chivalry was not dead. At least not in Rafe's book. She tucked the keys into her backpack and fixed a teasing smile on her face before turning to meet him.

"You know, Uncle Robbie installed a security camera back here. And the city put in an extra light. You don't have to wait and walk me to my car after closing every night." It was hard to miss the lack of an answering smile on his ruggedly sculpted features. "Especially when you've put in a long day like this one."

"It's no trouble." The flat response was a recitation of duty. Her heart squeezed at the exhaustion she heard in his gravelly tone, and she simply fell into step beside him when he took her elbow and walked her toward the beat-up Ford compact parked beside his shiny, supersize truck. "You warm enough in this?"

"I'm fine."

"I can buy you a new winter coat if you need one."

"No, you won't. And I don't."

"Damn it, Jose—are you going to argue every little thing I say to you tonight?"

"Whoa." Josie planted her feet, forcing him to halt. What the heck? She tipped her chin to try to decipher the sharp bite to his tone. "What's going on?"

A white cloud of breath formed in the chilly November air at his chest-deep sigh. "Sorry. I've got too many things running through my mind to be civil, I guess."

"Rafe?"

"Just walk."

She might have imagined the slight tremble she'd felt in his long fingers before they wound around the sleeve of her insulated jacket and resumed their pace across the parking lot. But she wasn't as concerned with the thinness of her thrift-store jacket as she was with her friend's cryptic remark. Rafe looked tired. It was that bone-deep kind of weariness that seeped into the soul and indicated a man who had seen and endured more than he should.

Although his stern face remained a mask just above her line of sight, Josie could see the signs. She was the kind of woman who noticed subtle details and read others the way most folks read a book. That talent came in handy working nights as a bartender, and she hoped to put those same skills to work once she completed her nursing degree next summer. Her senses were even more finely tuned when she cared about that person.

And Josie Nichols had cared about Rafe through a teenage crush, the loss of her father—a man they'd both loved—and the bond of adult friendship. In some ways, she was closer to Rafe Delgado than she was to any other person on the planet. But he'd made it clear his heart was off-limits to her, and so she'd buried those feelings of infatuation that had matured into something much more profound now that she was a twenty-five-year-old woman.

Except for times like this—when the hour was late and the night separated them from the rest of the world. When they were alone. When Rafe was hurting and the self-avowed loner needed someone and she knew she could help.

Josie could guess at the pain shading his amber brown eyes. She'd seen the tragic story played on the news over and over that evening. She'd listened to the sketchy details he and his friends on KCPD's SWAT

Team One had shared when they'd come in to drink a beer after this afternoon's deadly, heartbreaking stand-off against one of Kansas City's most violent gangs. And then, before they'd had any real opportunity to decompress from the stress of the day, his SWAT team had been called away to the scene of a bomb threat to help calm a restless crowd who feared a serial killer had struck again.

Rafe had every reason to be in a mood. An innocent boy had died today. And while Rafe and his team had saved dozens of lives, it was the one life he'd lost that stayed with him. She'd heard the speech before. The first time was the night ten years ago when Rafe, little more than a rookie patrol cop himself, had come to the house to tell Josie and her half brother, Patrick, that their father had been mowed down in the street by a group of bank robbers in their getaway car. He'd glossed over the fact that he and her father had stopped the armed thieves, protecting bystanders on the street and recovering hundreds of thousands of dollars in stolen money. Instead, he'd sat on the couch between her and Patrick, with barely a tear leaking from the corner of his red-rimmed eyes, even though she knew he felt as though he'd lost a father, too.

Rafe was thirty-four years old now, but little had changed. Saving lives was doing his job—losing a life was personal. But that damn pride and noble code of honor he lived by kept him from grieving properly. Kept him from dealing with the rage and frustration and guilt that must be eating him up inside.

"Rafe, stop." She halted beside his truck. She couldn't keep her hands to herself when she saw the muscle twitching beneath the stony frown of his expression. Reaching up, Josie cupped his jaw, soothing the tension she felt in him. "That boy didn't die because of you."

"No. He died in spite of me." The sensitive skin of Josie's palm prickled at the rasp of late-night beard stubble that abraded her skin as he snagged her wrist and pulled her hand away. "His name was Calvin Chambers. And I can't get his blood off my fingers."

She twisted her grip to capture his hands between both of hers, angling them up toward the street lamp, turning them over. "I don't see any blood."

And then the floodgates of emotions opened. He spun away, raking his fingers through his hair, leaving a mess of short, tobacco brown spikes in their wake. He paced into the shadows beyond the circle of light illuminating them. "It's stuck in my head. The blood was so warm and he was so cold. He had bullet holes in his leg and chest. I tried to stop the bleeding. I had to pitch my gloves and uniform, there was so much of it."

"Oh, my God. The news never said it was that bad." Josie squeezed her fingers around the strap of her backpack, seeking a little comfort herself. "That poor child."

"He was so young. Ten years old. Ten freaking years old." Rafe stepped back into the light, startling her. "What the hell was I doing—sittin' there while Calvin bled out?"

"Rafe." She'd seen him decked out in his SWAT gear—black uniform, flak vest, helmet, a handgun, a rifle and gear she didn't know the name for. "Horrible people who didn't give a damn about that little boy were shooting guns at cops. You broke up a gang, a drug ring. His killer was arrested. You weren't sitting there doing nothing. You were looking out for that boy."

"All I could do was hold him. I know what it feels like to be that young and that hurt. Nothing makes sense. All you know is fear and pain, and all you worry about is if it can possibly hurt any worse."

She watched his face contort as the grief welled up and he fought it back inside him. The anger, the self-recriminations, rolled off him in waves. Josie knew that not one whit of it was directed at her. He needed to vent, and listening was another skill in her survivor's repertoire. Instinctively, she drifted closer, slipping her hand beneath his jacket to rest it over his thumping heart. "I know you did everything you could to save him."

He covered her hand with his, squeezing almost too tightly as he held it against the stuttering expansion and contraction of his chest. "I'm trained to take action, Josie. I'm not supposed to sit still and tell a child lies like he's going to see his mama soon and everything will be all right." He slid his warm hand along her jaw, tipping her face to trace the tears that spilled over her cheek with the pad of his thumb, as if touching the evidence of her compassion and sorrow was the only way to acknowledge the anguish he felt. "I couldn't get to a proper med kit. I couldn't get an ambulance to him."

She turned to press a kiss into his palm. "Your captain said there was a lot of gunfire. You were pinned down."

"Captain Cutler wasn't in that alley with me. I was lucky to pull Calvin out of that backyard at all." He stroked his thumb across her cheek again, wiping away another tear. "And damn it—" Rafe's voice shook, "—he kept trying to thank me for protecting him. He was scared to death, yet he was foolish enough or brave enough to try to make me feel better." He stroked his fingers across her temple, tucking a long strand of hair behind her ear and smoothing it back into the ponytail at her nape. "He died in an alley. In a stranger's arms. Walking home from school. That's not right for any child."

Over the years she'd known Rafe, he'd occasionally hinted at the horrors of his own childhood. Something about today's tragic events must be resonating deep inside him, waking feelings he normally barricaded behind an internal layer of armor. "No. It's not."

He stroked his thumb across her bottom lip and paused, as if he'd felt the same electric shock she had. "Somebody else should have gone after him. Somebody else could have saved him."

"Rafe…" His need was waking something vital and primal and feminine deep inside her. "He couldn't have been in better hands."

"Damn protocol. Damn rules. I should have blasted my way out of that alley—"

"Others might have gotten hurt."

"—and gotten him to the hospital."

"Stop it, Rafe." Josie let her backpack slide off her shoulder and plop at her feet. She moved a step closer, framing his face between her hands. "Just stop."

He pulled his fingers through her long, dark ponytail, then flipped it behind her back. He smoothed his hands across her shoulders, touched his finger to the rip she'd mended in the sleeve of her jacket. She wondered at the tiny frissons of heat that followed his every touch. Josie no longer felt the nip of November dampness in the air. She no longer heard the whispers of traffic on the street at the front side of the bar, no longer knew the hour of night or the fatigue in her own body as Rafe leaned in and touched his forehead to hers. "When your dad taught me about being a cop, he didn't teach me how to…how to lose a child. I feel so damn helpless."

"You're tough, Rafe, but nobody's that tough." She gave him a little shake, worried at the raw loss shading his eyes. "Dad would be proud of the man you've become. He'd be proud of the cop you are."

His hands finally settled at her waist, his fingers biting into the flare of her hips as he pulled her close enough for their jeans to rustle together and new pressure points beneath her skin to awaken at the needy contact. "Your dad would have saved him."

Josie wound her arms around Rafe's neck, sliding her fingers beneath the soft collar of his leather jacket to find the smooth warmth of his skin to anchor herself to. "This isn't Dad all over again. You were the best chance Calvin Chambers had. If anyone could have saved him, it was you. At least he had someone strong and caring with him at the end. He wasn't alone." Tears burned in her throat and reduced her voice to a whisper. "How wonderful that you made him smile."

"If someone's going to die, I'm the go-to guy to have around, huh?"

"No, damn it, Rafe." Words weren't working. He couldn't hear her. He wouldn't hear. Rafe Delgado needed to feel the truth. "I'm so sorry you're hurting like this. Don't keep it in. It's okay to hurt."

She followed her instincts, doing the most natural, right thing she could think of, and kissed him. How many times, since she was fifteen years old, had she wanted to press her lips against Rafe's? How many lonely nights had she dreamed about turning their friendship into something more? But she'd always held back, settling for a peck on the cheek, treasuring a hug. But his emotions were too far off the chart tonight to settle for anything less than complete honesty between them.

"Shh." She kissed him again, lightly brushing her lips across his, testing the will of this coiled panther of a man, cooing sounds of desire and comfort in her throat.

Josie's lips parted as shock made him go still. His fingers aligned her hips with his. The heat of his body surrounded hers. Had she just broken some unspoken rule? Or did he understand she was giving him permission to kiss her back? Josie waited. Wanted. Dreamed.

Then, as if some understanding had snapped into place inside his head, Rafe inhaled a groaning breath and took over. He drove one thigh between hers and backed Josie against the truck. He slipped his tongue between her lips and deepened the kiss. She tasted the tang of beer on his tongue and the salty notes of tears from her own mouth.

With an impatient, throaty sigh, he unzipped her jacket and slipped his hand inside to squeeze her breast. The tender skin ignited beneath his touch and lit an ember deep in her core. Josie held on to his strong shoulders, her toes leaving the pavement as his knee wedged tighter, sparking flames that licked through her blood until they met up with his hands and mouth and consumed her in heat.

Rafe's breathy gasps matched her own. She was vaguely aware of one hand reaching beside her to open the truck door, while she was blatantly, eagerly aware of the other hand tugging at the buttons of her blouse until it could find its way inside to torment the aching nub of her breast through the lace of her bra.

The loneliness of Josie's solitary life—no mother, no father, a poor excuse for a brother, too much work and too much stress—evaporated beneath the greedy assault of Rafe's hands and mouth on her skin. He needed her. He needed *her*. The connection between them was ir-refutable and intense.

As her top veed open to the night air, and the chilly dampness bathed her in goose bumps, Rafe left her. "No. Don't stop."

But Rafe wasn't leaving, he was looking for a little more privacy. He tossed her bag inside and before Josie could follow his lead, he lifted her onto the seat, shutting the door behind him and following her across to the passenger side. With little heed for long legs and cramped quarters and layers of clothing, Rafe maneuvered her onto his lap. He tugged off his belt and placed his gun safely in the glove compartment as Josie's fingers tested the contrasts between his short, silky hair and the rougher texture of his stubbled jaw. And then she had his full attention again. Rafe slid his arms beneath her jacket and blouse and pulled her hard against him, his hands roaming at will against her skin, his mouth claiming hers. The urgency of every touch, every kiss, conveyed the depth of emotion that Rafe had been unable to speak.

Josie cracked open a little more of her battered heart and answered. This wasn't about slow seduction. It wasn't about finesse. It was about needing and caring, giving and taking.

"I don't ever want to have a child look at me that way again," Rafe rasped against her lips. "I don't want to hurt like this. I don't want to feel…"

"Shh. It's okay. Let it go."

With Josie's knees splayed on either side of Rafe's thighs, and the hard bulge of his zipper pulsing against the seam of her jeans, he left no doubt about what he was asking of her. "We never… I shouldn't…"

His face was buried against her neck, and he was shaking so hard with the effort to restrain himself that her body vibrated right along with his. But she could also feel the heat and moisture of the tears he blinked against her skin. She pulled away just far enough to hold his face and turn his golden-brown eyes to the dim moonlight. The tears she saw pooling there made the decision for her. Her heart couldn't say no.

"You know I've wanted this. Wanted to be more than friends." Josie reached down to unzip her jeans, to assure him of his welcome and her own desire.

He studied her face, looking as surprised as she by the unexpected passion and soul-deep empathy burning between them.

"It's okay, Rafe." She leaned in and kissed him. "We're okay."

And then Rafe began to move with the urgent

efficiency with which he defused bombs and took down bad guys. It was all fast and furious—a physical expression of every powerful emotion surging between them. Zippers crunched. His billfold came out. Clothes were pushed aside.

"I need you, Jose. I need you. I need…" Molding hands and desperate kisses made her blood drum through her veins. The heat rising inside her was almost unbearable. She could only hold on to his sturdy shoulders as he slid inside her, moving and rocking until they were both mindless with this physical, sensual outpouring of emotion.

"I love you, Rafe," she whispered as he crushed her in his arms and plunged inside her one last time, groaning with the release that she freely and willingly gave him.

HE SHOULD BE feeling better than this.

Rafe drew his fingers through the condensation forming on the side window of his truck and brushed the cool moisture across his feverish cheek. Oh, his body was well and truly satisfied—too spent and content to want one more thing. And those hated emotions that had raged through his system had dissipated under Josie's patient insistence and undeserved generosity.

She was snuggled up against his side in the truck now, her rumpled clothes refastened, her breathing slow and even. When he felt her stirring, he leaned over and pressed a kiss to the crown of her dark sable hair. When she tilted her chin and smiled at him, he knew what he was feeling.

Guilt.

He'd taken slaps across the face and a belt across his backside that didn't hurt as bad as this. He'd betrayed a friend tonight. Two of them. On the day Aaron had died, he'd made him a promise. Visiting his son in jail and boinking his daughter weren't exactly how he'd intended to honor Aaron's memory.

Some damn fine protector he turned out to be.

Josie's soft smile turned into a quizzical frown. "What are you thinking about?"

"Your dad." He shifted a little space between them, so that his thigh was no longer touching the tempting warmth of hers. "This wasn't my finest moment. I took advantage of that big heart of yours. I needed..." His deep sigh of remorse echoed in the truck. "I just needed."

"You needed to connect with someone who cared. Someone who would listen and let you feel what you needed to." She zipped her jacket and folded her arms across her middle. Was she cold? Rafe slid over to the steering wheel and pulled out his keys to start the truck and turn on the heater.

"Yeah, well, I should have stopped at talking."

"Not your strong suit," she teased. "You've always been a more physical being."

"I told Aaron I would always take care of you. Tonight, I just used you."

"That's insulting."

"Josie."

"Hey, I'm not a naive girl anymore. You're not my first, Rafe, so I knew what I was doing. It's not like you forced me."

"Damn close."

He found her crystal-blue eyes across the cab, saw them blanch wide and then darken. She turned in her seat, twisting the argument back on him. "You would have stopped if I'd asked. But I didn't want you to stop. Sometimes a relationship works that way. One partner needs more than the other at a given time. It's a mutual give and take."

"We don't have a relationship like that."

"Would that be such a bad thing?"

Oh, yeah. He was not relationship material. Definitely not with his former partner's daughter. After tonight, he might not even be friend material. "My emotions were out of control. That was a mistake."

She sat up ramrod straight, her Irish temper coloring her cheeks. "Making love was a mistake? Or feeling something was a mistake?"

Making love? She thought that wham-bam, thank-you, ma'am, was how it was supposed to be between a man and a woman? Just what kind of jerks had she been dating, who hadn't shown her how good it could be if a man took his time and… Ah, hell. *Put on the brakes. Don't go there.*

He squeezed his hands around the steering wheel. "I'm sorry, Jose. I made a promise to your dad to take care of you. I'm sorry."

"Stop apologizing. I always figured it would be intense with you. That's kind of exciting. And you know I…care about you."

And he cared about her. But he couldn't keep trouble away or screen those jerks or even make sure she got safely to her car when she worked too late if his senses were blurred by his emotions and his focus was distracted by long legs and lush lips and that gorgeous fall of dark hair. He could hardly do right by her if *he* was the trouble. "Look, I already failed Patrick. I couldn't keep him off drugs and out of jail. I don't want to mess up what we have."

"Rafe, what about what I want?"

He opened his door and stepped out into the night. The bracing air filled his lungs and cleared his head of her lingering scent. "You've got class in the morning and you need to get home. I need to get back to the precinct garage and get the SWAT van cleaned up and refitted for our next call."

She grabbed her backpack and climbed out her side of the truck. "You have to do that tonight?"

Oh, yeah. He needed to get his hands busy doing something besides itching to reach for Josie again. He needed to busy his mind with a task where he didn't have to second-guess his every move. "I'm a jerk, okay?"

"Please stop. It hurts me to hear you talk like this."

"I never wanted to hurt you. I don't want things to change between us. I want you to be able to trust me. I *need* you to trust me. Nothing like that will ever happen again. I promise." After she unlocked her car, he opened the door for her and waited while she slid behind the wheel. Man, he wished she'd let him pick out something more reliable than this rattletrap for her. At least she let him change the oil and keep the motor tuned up and running as well as a beater car like this one could. "Go on, I'll wait to make sure your car starts. I'll see you next time you work at the Shamrock."

She turned the key. Once the engine growled to life,

he started to leave. But Josie put out her arm to keep him from shutting the door. "Just for the record? You weren't a jerk for making love to me. *Now* you're being a jerk."

Of that he had no doubt.

He jumped back as she slammed the door, knowing he deserved worse. Once inside his truck, he followed her out of the parking lot but turned in the opposite direction toward his condo. He'd better be keeping a lot more than a few miles of physical distance between them. What the hell was he thinking? That was the problem—he hadn't been thinking.

Josie's skin was cool and pale in the frosty moonlight. Her touch was so gentle, so certain. He'd gotten more drunk on her lips than the beer she'd served him earlier that night. And her body—her tall, lithe, sweet body with those long legs snugged around him...

"Damn." He was breaking out in a sweat that had nothing to do with the heater in his truck.

Josephine Erin Nichols was his friend. His unofficial ward. His penance for letting his friend and mentor die ten years ago.

She was pretty and kind and sexy and funny, and strictly off-limits. And yet, for several mindless minutes tonight, she'd been everything he needed. Exactly what he needed.

He'd been a rutting bull who'd taken advantage of her friendship and compassionate nature. Hell, he'd barely gotten a condom on and hadn't even asked if she was on the pill. In his saner days before this one, he hadn't wanted to know if his sweet, hardworking buddy was sleeping with anyone. She was either working one of several part-time jobs, studying or going to school, so he knew she didn't have much time to date. He hadn't even had the presence of mind to make sure that she'd found the completion he had.

He was a jerk. A lonesome, selfish, let-friends-and-children-die-on-his-watch jerk. He'd been on his own since high school for a reason. And it wasn't just because he'd severed all ties with his worthless parents. He'd become obsessed with his job and the sweetheart he'd been engaged to had left him. He was alone because he couldn't make a relationship with a woman work.

But he could find solace in her beautiful, willing body.

Rafe picked up speed and merged into the late-night traffic that was mostly big rigs at this time of night on Interstate 435, and waited for the lightning bolt of her late father's spirit, or his own troubled conscience, to strike him dead.

Chapter Two

"You didn't bring me any cigarettes?"

Josie Nichols let the accusation in her half brother Patrick's tone sink in and curdle with the nausea already rolling in her stomach. "By the end of this summer, I'll be a registered nurse, and I'm not going to support such an unhealthy, expensive habit. Anyway, you promised me you were quitting."

"That was last month." Patrick leaned back from the plastic table in the KCPD detention center where she'd come to visit him between classes at UMKC and her nightly shift at the Shamrock Bar. His blue eyes narrowed as he brushed his dark hair off his forehead. Their black-Irish looks were about the only thing she had in common with what was left of her so-called family. "I've got pressures in here that keep me on edge, and a couple of smokes could go a long way toward making me feel better. Besides, they're like cash in here."

Josie slipped her hand below the tabletop, gently rubbing at the small bump on her belly, trying to coax some cooperation from her stomach. "What do you need to buy in jail?"

"Protection. Weed. Private time in the shower." He leaned forward again, propping his elbows on the table. She noticed the sinuous lines of a snake circling his forearm. Great. He'd given himself another tattoo. Sanitary considerations aside, their father would be so proud. Not.

"Are you in some kind of trouble?"

He paused for a moment, blinked, then sat back, silencing whatever he'd been about to share. "No more than usual. You bring me cigarettes next time you come."

Although her regular bouts of morning sickness had passed, long times between snacks and stress like this visit could easily trigger that unsettled feeling. Josie hadn't told Patrick about the baby. She hadn't told anyone beyond their Uncle Robbie—who'd found her in the Shamrock's restroom kneeling over the toilet two afternoons in a row, and said he recognized the signs from his own dear late Maureen—and the nurse practitioner-midwife who was taking care of her. The midwife was paid to be discreet, and no one kept a secret better than Robbie, even though he'd pestered her time and again to give him the father's name so he could "set the ruddy bastard straight."

Her relationship with Rafe had tanked after that night in the parking lot. Oh, he was just as protective as ever—annoyingly so—showing up to escort her to her car after work, coming over to her apartment to fix her car when it wouldn't run. But he'd turned into such a bear, nit-picking her every decision as if she was a child, arguing over trivial things, refusing to discuss anything deep or meaningful. He put in as many hours with his SWAT team—training, answering calls, volunteering for off-duty assignments—as she worked in a day, leaving them no time to sit down to talk and reconnect. Rafe had once again become the loner she'd first met all those years ago—afraid to attach himself to anyone, afraid to care.

Josie splayed her fingers, cradling the precious life growing inside her even more carefully. Sooner or later, her secret could no longer be hidden beneath loose clothes. But if Rafe couldn't deal with her in a healthy, reasonable way, then how would he deal with a child? If nightmares of dying children and his own abuse growing up still haunted his sleep, then why would he want one of his own? While she had no doubt that Rafe would do right by her once she found the courage to tell him, she knew his support would be all about providing money or a name or whatever the kid needed that didn't involve any emotional commitment.

If he couldn't or wouldn't love her or their child, then how could they ever hope to be a real family?

So Josie intended to treasure this baby all by herself, delaying the fight and the blame and the guilt Rafe would surely heap upon himself once he found out. She'd never known a man to hurt as deeply as Rafe Delgado did. He'd suffered so much loss in his life that he trusted duty and honor more than his heart. Or hers. So Josie kept her secret.

Yeah. Aaron Nichols would be real proud of both his children.

"I brought you the magazines you asked for." Even

the seedy ones she'd swallowed her pride to purchase at the convenience store for him. "Happy Birthday. I'd have baked you a cake and brought that, too, if it wasn't such a stereotype. You know, hiding a hacksaw inside it."

But Patrick didn't laugh with her, or even smile. Or thank her.

Instead, he signaled for the guard at the door, indicating the visit was over.

"I love you, Patrick. Be good. I want you to make your parole and get out of here…" *by the time the baby comes.* So she wouldn't be quite so alone. But Patrick didn't care about her wishes any more than Rafe did. "I want you out of here soon."

"Me, too. Bring me those cigarettes."

No "I love you." No "thanks, sis." No "goodbye."

Tears blurred her vision as the guard released him from the room and another escorted him to his cell. Josie pulled a tissue from her pocket and quickly dabbed them away, wishing she could blame the sudden sense of loss and loneliness she felt on her fluctuating hormones. She sniffed loudly enough to embarrass herself and glanced over at the two men across the room, shaking hands at their table. The prisoner in the orange jumpsuit seemed startled by the consideration that her own brother hadn't even shown her. But the man in the suit and tie—his lawyer, most likely—said a few words that calmed his client. A few gentle words, some show of caring and support would have been enough for her as well.

The tears welled up again and Josie quickly turned away to dab her eyes and collect the sack she'd brought

Patrick's magazines in. Ashamed by her weakness, she stood and hurried toward the exit. She'd taken only three steps before plowing into the attorney's chest.

Instinctively, her hand went to her abdomen and she backed away. "I'm sorry. I wasn't looking."

She looked up to offer him an apologetic smile, and would have grinned outright when she saw his toupee sitting slightly askew on his forehead. But there was a blank look behind his glasses, something so cold and devoid of emotion in his light-colored eyes, even more so than Rafe's, that her smile died and she took a second step back.

"My fault entirely, ma'am." He smiled. But even that outward gesture of civility didn't reach his eyes. He was wiping his fingers with a crisp, white handkerchief. And was that…? Were those drops of blood she glimpsed before he tucked the crisp white cloth back into his pocket?

"Are you all right?"

"No harm done." He nodded to the guard and reached for the open door. "After you."

Maybe her hormones were out of whack and her imagination was working overtime. He'd probably suffered something as simple as a nosebleed. Lord knew the air in this place was dry as a bone. "Thanks."

But a gurgling sound behind her caused Josie to stop and turn. And go on instant alert.

The prisoner had slumped over the table, clutching his throat.

"Wait a minute. Is he…? Is your client all right?" When she spun around, the man had disappeared and the guard was closing the door behind him. "Guard!"

The uniformed black man hurried right behind her. The prisoner was shaking now.

"He's convulsing. Help me get him to the floor." All of Josie's training kicked in as she cleared the man's throat and turned him onto his side.

The guard was on his radio, calling for backup, while she checked the prisoner's thready pulse and fixed, pinpoint stare of his pupils. He wasn't breathing. His heart was stopping. She had nothing but her hands to help him. He needed a tracheotomy. Now. "Do you have a knife?"

Fifteen minutes later, the medic on staff at the detention center pronounced what Josie already knew.

"He's dead."

She wiped the blood from her hands and dashed over to the corner of the room to empty her stomach.

THE NOISE OF clacking pool balls and TV broadcasts and dozens of conversations was particularly grating tonight. Josie waited a moment in the Shamrock Bar's walk-in freezer, counting the clouds formed by each breath, savoring the utter quiet of insulated walls and cold, heavy air.

But she was already shivering. She'd be hypothermic if she waited in here long enough for her headache to pass.

Ignoring the throbbing inside her skull and the twinge in her lower back, she lifted a crate of bottled beer off the shelf and backed her hip into the door release. The noise assaulted her eardrums the moment the door swung open. But this was rent money, or maybe that oak crib that was in such good shape at the thrift store. So she'd sucked up the pain and pasted a smile on her face by the time she left the back hallway and pushed through the swinging door that took her behind the Shamrock's polished walnut bar.

"There you are, girlie." Uncle Robbie plucked the crate from her hands and winked one crinkling blue eye. His robust Irish voice warmed with concern. "I wondered where you'd got to. Everything all right?"

Josie nodded, resisting the urge to touch her belly out here where the other staff and customers could see. "I just needed some fresh air."

"You know I'll give you all the time off you need." His silvering dark curls bobbed up and down as he cradled the beer on his hip and opened the cooler behind the bar to drop the bottles in one by one. "You only have to ask."

Josie eyed the two waitresses at their station, waiting to have trays filled, and took note of the customers standing two and three deep behind the green vinyl bar stools while Lance, another part-time student bartender hurried back and forth. Robbie Nichols was short-staffed, as usual, his nose for business not nearly as reliable as the charity in his heart.

"Who called in sick tonight?" Josie asked, answering the high sign from one of the waitresses and pulling two pilsners from the rack above the bar to draw a pair of beers.

Robbie's thick stomach jiggled as he laughed. "You know me too well, girlie. Enrico called, said he was under the weather. Odds are that's a lie, but what can I do?"

It was a bet she wouldn't take. Knowing Enrico

Gonzalez, he was probably under the sheets with his girlfriend—or sleeping the evening away after staying too late at her apartment the night before. Josie set the beers on the tray and took the next server's order for a round of whiskey shots.

How was she ever going to leave Robbie to his own devices long enough to finish her nursing practicum at the Truman Medical Center or go on maternity leave? "Why don't you let me run this for a few minutes, and you go in the office and call Allison to see if she can come in and help out. You really need to fire Enrico and hire someone more reliable, too, so we don't get shorthanded like this again."

"You sure got your daddy's level head, didn't ye?" He crushed the box between his meaty hands and leaned in to kiss her cheek. "Fine. I'll go call. But I don't want to come back and find you lifting anything heavier than that whiskey bottle, understand?"

Josie grinned and shooed him toward the swinging door. "Yes. Now go before we lose any more customers for being too slow to serve them."

"I'll wait as long as you need me to, Miss Nichols." Josie set the shot glass she'd just filled on the tray and turned to the red-haired man in a suit and tie sitting at the corner of the bar. Something about him seemed familiar, but with the chaotic distractions going on all around her, she couldn't immediately place him. He pulled a leather wallet from his suit coat and flashed a brass and blue enamel badge. "My name's Spencer Montgomery. I'm a detective with KCPD."

Maybe that's what she recognized. Being located just a few blocks from KCPD's Fourth Precinct station, the

Shamrock Bar drew the majority of its customers from cops and KCPD support staff. He must be a returning customer. "What can I get you, Detective Montgomery?"

"A cup of coffee is all right now. I'm on the clock."

Josie went to the counter behind the bar to pour him a mug of coffee. "Here you go. The coffee is always on the house."

But his light green eyes warned her that he wasn't really here for something to drink. "When the baseball game rush is over, I'd like to ask you a few questions."

"About what?"

"About the murder you witnessed today."

AT 1:42 A.M., Josie locked the door behind her and turned to face the Shamrock's parking lot. What she needed after this endless day and longer night was a hug and a hot shower.

What she got was Rafe Delgado.

The springtime air was cool and pleasant, but a shiver rippled down Josie's spine when his truck door opened and he strode out across the parking lot to meet her. He was still wearing his SWAT uniform, crisp black from head to toe, with only *KCPD* and his last name embroidered in white on his chest pocket, the badge on his belt and a gun strapped to his thigh to break up his lean, dangerous look.

"Are you on duty?" she asked, pulling her shoulders back, bracing for another impersonal, duty-motivated meeting. "How many times have I told you I can get someone else to walk me to my car when you're working?"

"And who's that going to be?" He propped his hands on his hips and scanned the nearly empty lot from side to side. He glanced up at the dark windows on the building's second floor. "Did Robbie already turn in? He should walk you out."

"He would if I asked. He's on the phone with my cousin, Susan, back in Ireland." She could do a little contemptuous scanning of her own, up and down his tall, rangy build. "Besides, he knew you'd be here like clockwork, so why bother?"

Rafe no longer took her arm when he walked her to her car, but instead fell into step beside her as she headed for her Fiesta. "Why the hell didn't you tell me you'd gone to see Patrick today?"

Josie bristled at his tone. "It's his birthday. I always go."

"I would have gone with you."

Like having him lurking in the corner, standing watch over her, would have made the day go any better. "You weren't invited."

His breath seethed between his teeth. "So now I hear you're running a trauma unit there?"

Josie stopped in her tracks, cinching the straps of her backpack in tight fists as she tilted her chin to meet his downturned gaze. She stood five foot seven, and he could still make her feel small when he glowered like that. "Not tonight, Rafe. Just get back in your truck and wait for me to drive away."

"Do you know who that was you tried to save?"

"I was told his name was Kyle Austin. Apparently, he's part of some wealthy family with good lawyers who got him into the same security facility as Patrick. I guess money can't save your life, though, can it."

His clean-shaven face tightened with a stony look. "Austin is the man who was masquerading as the Rich Girl Killer. He's a stalker. An embezzler. A kidnapper. He tried to kill Charlotte Mayweather and Trip."

Flinching in surprise, Josie quickly processed the names. Trip was Rafe's friend, a fellow SWAT cop. He'd been hospitalized for most of a month after nearly dying while rescuing the reclusive Mayweather heiress from her kidnappers. "I thought the name was familiar. But I had no idea who he was. Has Trip recovered from his wounds yet?"

"He's on vacation with Charlotte right now. He reports back for duty next Monday." Rafe leaned in ever so slightly. "Just think how dangerous a man has to be to go nose to nose with a cop with Trip's skills. You don't want to be messing with a bastard like that."

Bastard status aside, Josie had a calling. "He was dying."

"There are people on staff to help—"

"*I* was there to help."

"You can't save everyone, Josie." She glared up at him. He knew he was at the top of her list of lost causes. "You need to stop trying. You're going to get hurt."

Tell me about it. Josie pulled her keys from her backpack and headed toward her car. She was tired, upset, hungry and in no mood to be reminded of that foolish night when she'd mistaken physical intimacy for an emotional connection. She'd opened up her heart that night—and Rafe had closed up his. Lesson learned.

"It's over and done with, Rafe. Detective Montgomery

said he had ruled me out as a suspect in Mr. Austin's death, so I probably won't have to talk about it ever again." She glanced over her shoulder at him. "Hint, hint."

"Back up. When did you talk to Spencer Montgomery?"

He knew the red-haired detective? Josie shrugged as they reached her car. "He came to the bar tonight. He's investigating Kyle Austin's death as a homicide."

"He doesn't deal with jail-cell murders." Rafe's hand on hers stopped her from sticking her key into the lock. "He's investigating the Rich Girl Killer serial murders and related deaths. Does he think you know something?"

"I don't know." For a moment, Josie imagined the warmth seeping from Rafe's hand into hers was meant to comfort. But she wisely pulled away. "At first he thought I might have had something to do with Austin's death."

"Montgomery's an idiot."

"No." Josie remembered the unabashed perusal of those pale green eyes. "I think he's really smart. I thought he was going to accuse me of slitting Austin's throat."

"What?"

"I had to perform an emergency tracheotomy. The medic, he was there—he said I did everything just right." Memories of all the blood she'd washed from her hands and blouse, and the nerves she'd squashed down so that she could offer the help he'd needed, squeezed like a fist inside her, intensifying the headache and sour stomach she'd been fighting all day. "But that wasn't it. I mean, he took a statement, like the officer and medic at the jail did. But Detective Montgomery had me brainstorm a list of poisons for him that could cause the anaphylactic shock—that's um, paralysis of his airways—that killed Mr. Austin."

"He could get that info online or out of a book."

"He already did. I saw his notepad. He had a list of poisons already written down."

Rafe braced one hand against the roof of her car and glanced up into the moonless sky before muttering a curse and swinging his gaze back down to her. "Did he accuse you of anything?"

Josie shook her head. "Not outright. But he sure made me feel guilty about letting Austin die."

Rafe's hand moved from the car to her shoulder, his hard expression changing as he gave her a gentle squeeze. "You didn't let anybody die. Montgomery was out of line."

Josie swayed on her feet, drawn to the warmth and security of Rafe's chest. But she didn't want to open up and be cast aside again. No matter that he claimed the distance he'd maintained these past six months was for her own good, the distance was there. And she was too weary, too wary, to breach it. She twisted away to unlock her car and toss her backpack across the front seat. "So now you're on my side? You can't have it both ways, Rafe. You can't lecture me about taking risks and then think you can be there to pick up the pieces when that risk fails."

His arms flew out in the air on either side of her, his frustration stamped on every inch of his tall frame. "I don't know how to talk to you anymore. I'm just trying to take care of you."

"We'll be just fine."

He grabbed the door when she tried to close it. "We?"

Oh, what a mighty slip of the tongue. There was no way to hide the truth from those dark, ever-watchful eyes now. She leaned back in the seat and pulled up the tails of her untucked blouse to reveal the elastic waistband of her maternity jeans hugging the small bump on her belly.

The dome light of the car revealed everything she wanted him to see. "You're pregnant?"

She tugged her blouse back into place and inserted the key in the ignition. "Brilliant deduction. And you're not even a detective."

"How far along are you?"

"Do the math, Rafe."

His strong arm kept her from closing the door. He stepped into the triangle between the door and the car and squatted down, forcing her to look straight into those suspicious amber eyes. "It's mine?"

Did he really think she had the time or inclination to be sleeping around? "It's yours."

"Why didn't you tell me?" His voice was little more than a husky whisper in the night.

Josie gripped the steering wheel, fighting the dueling urges to scoot away across the seat or to soothe that pulse beating along his tightly clenched jaw. "It hasn't exactly been business as usual between us lately. You changed that night. It's hard to confide in someone who snaps at me every chance he gets."

"I don't—" He had no room to argue there. "I've

seen the worst the world has to offer, Josie—and some of that's rubbed off on me. Maybe a lot of it. I wouldn't inflict what I've seen and who I am on anybody. Your dad knew that about me. That's why he wanted me to guard you from the dangers that are out there. It's the same reason he knew we shouldn't be together."

She wouldn't let him off that easily. "He didn't want us together because I was only fifteen years old back then. That's hardly the case now."

"I gave him my word."

"You worry too much about keeping your word to Dad." She swallowed hard, feeling a familiar pinch of loneliness. But she had to be strong for her son or daughter. In three months' time she wouldn't be alone anymore. "I know you loved him as much as I did, Rafe. I admire your loyalty, but he's gone. You'd do better to devote yourself to someone who's actually alive."

"Is that what you want? You want me to marry you?" He reached inside the car and Josie instinctively pulled her hands from the wheel and hugged her arms around her belly. The movement wasn't lost on Rafe. She could see it in his eyes—she was shielding her baby from him. "You know what kind of childhood I had. How I feel about…having kids."

"Oh, I know."

At last, he drew his hand away. "Are you giving the baby up? Keeping it?"

"I'm keeping Junior." She'd never considered any other option. "But don't worry. I absolve you of all responsibility. I'll sign papers if you want. I don't want anything from you. Just think of this baby as all mine. I do."

HE STOOD IN the shadows, waiting nearly thirty minutes for the cop sitting in his truck to quit cursing and banging his steering wheel, and then staring out into the darkness as though he might be holding back tears. Whatever Josie Nichols had said to him had clearly upset him.

Only after the black-suited cop had started the engine and peeled out of the parking lot, still fighting whatever the bad news had been, did he emerge from behind the Dumpster and walk to the vehicle he'd parked two blocks down the street. He pulled his handkerchief from his pocket, squirted it with a splash of breath spray and held the minty scent over his nose, trying to dispel the acrid stench from his hiding place that lingered in his nostrils.

Officer Mood Swing had thwarted his plan to make quick work of the situation that had developed. But his ongoing research and his patience in the shadows had paid off in other invaluable ways. He'd quickly learned Josie Nichols's nighttime routine. The fat uncle would be of no consequence—he'd taken the whiskey bottle upstairs to his apartment after closing the bar. But the big-brother cop could be as problematic as the extra security around the hospital where Miss Nichols spent most of her days.

He pressed the remote on his key chain as he approached his vehicle, pocketed the handkerchief as he found fresher air to breathe, and pulled a pack of cigarettes from his coat pocket. It was a nasty habit, one he indulged only when he needed to calm himself, when he needed to think. And he definitely needed to think now.

KCPD was closing in on him. Every time he wrapped up a loose end, another thread in his plan unraveled. They'd kept him from knowing the satisfaction of squeezing the life from his last two victims. And he was hungry for revenge now. Aching with the blood-pumping need to destroy the last two women who had denied him what was rightfully his.

He could see their faces now, telling him no, apologizing. As if *I'm sorry* made everything all right. His heart raced in his chest and his breathing went shallow as he remembered the humiliation. He'd been punished for his failures, punished his whole life for being different, for not being rich enough or powerful enough to earn his place in their world.

He stumbled over the curb and caught himself on the hood of the van. *Stupid, stupid boy!*

"Shut up," he muttered, remembering the fists and the torture, remembering how he'd suffered all because a woman had denied him what should have been his. "Shut up!"

Hearing his own voice echoing off the brick and stone buildings surrounding him brought him to his senses. He inhaled deeply on his cigarette, letting the nicotine sink into his lungs and blood, finding the calm he needed before grinding it out in the street beneath his foot.

Remembering his training, remembering to never leave one trace of DNA, one clue to connect him to any one place or crime, he carefully picked up the squished butt and climbed into the van. After disposing of the butt in the ashtray with the other two cigarettes he'd smoked, he picked up the digital camera from the seat beside him and turned it on to scroll through the pictures of his victims. It was a trip down memory lane that made him smile.

He'd paid far too dearly for not handling those four women as a younger man. But now Valeska Gallagher was dead. He clicked to a new picture. Gretchen Cosgrove was dead. And another. Audrey Kline and Charlotte Mayweather would be dead as soon as he could devise the right plan.

He just needed time.

Patience.

And a plan.

A self-important gang leader had ignored his instructions and botched his efforts to kill Audrey. Kyle Austin's interference had kept him from killing Charlotte. And now both men were dead.

There was only one thing standing in the way of his success now. Another woman.

Finding her name in the prison visitors' log when the guards had rushed in to help Kyle Austin had been easy enough. Sister of a druggie, and anyone with an arrest record was easy to trace. He'd found Patrick Nichols's information online, and saw that, ironically, the inconsequential inmate was the son of a slain cop. All the newspaper stories about Aaron Nichols's heroic death had led him straight to the Shamrock Bar.

And Josie.

He scrolled ahead to the last few pictures on his screen. Her long ponytail would give him something to hold onto if he decided to kill her with his hands. But then he was equally skilled with poisons and rifles. And he hadn't forgotten the bomb-making skills his father had taught him.

Josie Nichols wasn't his usual victim. She wasn't rich and she had no family, of influence or not, to speak of.

But she'd seen his face.

Even with his disguise, she'd been too close. He'd read the suspicion in her eyes. He'd seen the imprint of a memory being made.

Oh, how his fingers itched to wipe that look from her eyes.

It was only a matter of time before KCPD linked him to Kyle Austin's murder this afternoon—only a matter of time before Miss Nichols gave her description and some lucky cop spotted him. For years he'd been faceless. But now Josephine Nichols could look at him in a lineup or a courtroom and say, *That's the man I saw. He's your killer.* And then he'd be put in prison. Reunited with his father and uncles who'd left him for dead in a hospital emergency room long ago.

Josie Nichols could give him a face. She could take his freedom away. She could stop him before his retribution was complete.

And no woman could ever be allowed to have that kind of power over him again.

One way or another, Josie Nichols had to die.

Chapter Three

"I don't recognize any of the men in these pictures," Josie confessed, feeling as frustrated as the red-haired detective pacing the length of the interview room where he had her going through book after book of mug shot photos. "If one of these men is your killer, then maybe my memory's not as good as I thought."

But Spencer Montgomery didn't like that answer. He pulled the one she'd just closed back off the stack and opened it in front of her. "Are you sure? Look again."

"No." She shoved the book away, not sure if she wanted to throw it at Detective Montgomery or beg his dark-haired partner, Nick Fensom, who was sitting calmly at the far end of the conference table to say something. Ultimately, she took a deep breath, rubbed her tummy beneath the edge of the table to soothe the distress that was agitating both her stomach and the baby, and defended herself in a rational tone. "None of these men are the guy I saw wiping the blood off his hands just before Kyle Austin died. Those eyes? I'll never forget them. He's not here."

She thought she was coming in this morning to sign her statement about the events she'd seen Friday after visiting with Patrick. She had no idea these two detectives wanted to grill her up one side and down the other because they believed she'd come face-to-face with someone they'd dubbed The Rich Girl Killer.

She wanted to remind them that she'd come here of her own volition, trying to be the good citizen her father had taught her to be, despite the suspicions they'd initially thrown her way after Kyle Austin's death. She also wanted to remind them that she was already late for her shift at the Truman Medical Center where she was finishing up her nurse's training. And although her supervisor was married to a forensic scientist who worked for the police department, and said she understood such things, Josie didn't want any marks—like a lack of punctuality—to show up on her record.

Finally, the silent detective at the far end of the table spoke up. "Maybe he's never been arrested and he's not in the KCPD or State Patrol database. Do you want to try the FBI database?"

Josie's gaze shot to the clock on the wall. "How many pictures is that?"

Detective Fensom offered her a wry smile. "Too many to look at today, ma'am. But it might be worth forwarding your description to the Kansas City Bureau office to see if they pull any pix for you to look at on a later date."

Josie grabbed her backpack from the chair beside her. "So I can go?"

"One last thing." Detective Montgomery flipped through the papers in his folder and pulled out a copy of an enlarged image of a high-school yearbook page. He slapped it on the table in front of her and pointed to the picture of a boy with wiry hair, an acne-scarred chin and thick glasses. "Is that him?"

Leaning in, Josie studied the picture more closely and compared it to the man with the toupee she'd seen Friday. "Well, the man I saw looked fifteen years older—maybe because his hairline was receding, almost like arrow points. The cheekbones were different, the jawline more pronounced." She squinted, focusing in on the glasses he wore. The lenses distorted their size, but, "The eyes are the same." Josie leaned back, hugging her bag over her belly. There was something cold, something disconnected and eerily familiar in those pale eyes. She looked up at the detectives. "Is this him?"

"At least we're right about our Donny Kemp theory," Montgomery said to Fensom. Then he looked down to answer her. "This is what our suspect looked like when he was in high school. We believe he's had plastic surgery and has changed his identity more than once in the ten years since. If we can link Donny Kemp to whoever he is now—"

"The man I saw."

"—then we won't be chasing a shadow anymore. We could finally bring this guy in."

She glanced over at the computer composite a police artist had pieced together from her description of Kyle Austin's killer. The same cold eyes, masked behind a different pair of glasses, looked back at her and she shivered. "Am I in any danger?"

"All you've done is look at a ten-year-old photo. If we bring this guy in, and you identify him, we'll put you in a safe house until his case goes to trial. Otherwise..."

he pulled out the statement she'd signed earlier, folded it up and tucked it into the inside pocket of his jacket, "you're listed as a Jane Doe informant in my report."

"And I've talked to the prison about expunging your name from their files," Fensom added. "You won't even be in the M.E.'s report on Kyle Austin's death. Until we find him and arrest him, he has no reason to see you as a threat."

She pointed to the computer-generated picture. "Are you sure?"

Spencer Montgomery crossed to the door and opened it, indicating she was finally free to go. "I'd recommend practicing common sense when it comes to your personal safety, but I think extreme measures would only raise a red flag at this point. You be sure to contact us if you think of anything else, or if you do feel threatened in any way. You have my card, Miss Doe."

Miss Doe. Not Josie or Miss Nichols. She hunched her shoulders and lowered her head as she faced the bustle in and around the maze of cubicles on the detectives' division floor. As long as none of them knew why she was here, as long as Donny Kemp—or whoever he'd become—never learned her name, she'd be perfectly safe.

Josie took a deep breath and headed toward the elevators. She could do this. It was right to do this. Friday, she'd tried to save a man's life and had failed. Today, she'd confirmed the police's suspicions about the identity of a serial killer. Tomorrow...

Junior rolled onto her bladder and suddenly, Josie had to focus on finding the nearest bathroom.

This baby was her tomorrow. The precious life

growing inside her meant she wasn't alone in the world anymore. Rafe Delgado might regret the night they'd created this miracle, but she didn't.

Her only regret was that the baby would probably drive the final wedge between her and Rafe, ending whatever relationship they had left.

Just as she was about to push the elevator call button, the light for the fourth floor lit up and the doors slid open. Her heart shriveled when she spotted the five officers inside, outfitted in special black uniforms, weapons and gear that made them look as though they were marching into battle. It was useless to try to turn away, useless to duck her head and pretend she didn't know these regulars from the Shamrock.

Captain Cutler strode off first, tipping the bill of his hat. "Miss Nichols."

Trip Jones filled the opening, grinned, then stooped down to give her a hug. "Hey, Josie. Good to see you."

Alex Taylor winked. "Hey, Josie."

Miranda Murdock, the newest member of SWAT Team One, even offered a polite nod. "Hello."

Josie summoned the patience and strength to trade *hi's* and hugs and *how are you's* as the first four officers moved on past her.

But then Rafe was standing between the elevator doors, his grim, dark eyes sweeping over her.

"What are you all doing here?" she asked.

And then his hand was on her elbow, pulling her to one side, away from the criss-cross of traffic entering and exiting the floor. His fingers had burned through the cotton of her loose-fitting scrubs jacket by the time he'd turned her into the doorway of a closed office and released her. "Monday morning roll call," Rafe explained. "What are *you* doing here? Is something wrong?"

With her back pressed to the door it was hard to see anything beyond the dimensions of his chest, hard to stand her ground and tilt her chin and remind him that he didn't have any proprietary claim over her actions anymore. "I came in to sign my witness statement for Detectives Montgomery and Fensom."

He glanced away and shoved his fingers through his hair, leaving the short, tobacco-brown spikes in a mess that she would have smoothed back into place for him six months ago. Yet when he faced her again, the only message stamped on his face was a warning. "Don't get involved with this case. We're talking a serial killer here."

She curled her fingers into her palms, fighting the urge to touch him, to soothe his concern. "Would you back down from doing your duty? Or did you learn different lessons from my father?"

"I'm trained to do what I do."

"And you don't think I've learned a few survival skills over the years, with the people I know and the things I've been through?"

He shook his head. "I don't want you to get hurt, Jose. I care about you."

"Yeah, just not enough to do something about it."

With that, Rafe drew back, taking his heat and charged energy with him. "I'll admit you gave me a good shock Friday night. But you know I'll take care of the baby—medical bills, day care—whatever you need."

Feeling a bit of pity that he could see no joy, nor feel any hope, at the miracle they'd created together, she reached up and brushed her fingertips across his smooth, warm jaw. His pulse leaped beneath her touch and she smiled sadly. "My brave, noble, do-the-right-thing Rafe. That's the big issue, isn't it? I don't think you understand what I really need." She pulled her hand down to her distended belly. "What *we* really need. And if you do, I don't know if you'll ever be able to give it."

His gaze followed her hand down, then back up to look her in the eye. "Jose, don't do this. Keep yourself and the kid safe. Montgomery can find another way to catch this guy."

Knowing his concern for her safety was genuine, yet knowing that depending on him would only resurrect feelings that were too painful to bear right now, Josie put her hand on his chest and pushed him back out of her space. "It's not your call to make, Rafe. Now you've got a meeting to get to and I'm late for my practicum. Goodbye."

It was the most unnatural thing in the world to turn her back on Rafe and walk away. The baby seemed to know it, too. Junior shifted inside her, in Josie's mind, trying to reach for Daddy and the heat and strength and security Rafe had in such abundance. The little traitor. She was trying to be strong enough for both of them, trying to save them both the heartache of wanting Rafe Delgado.

Sensing that Rafe was standing there, watching her every step of the way, Josie pushed the elevator's call button and waited. The swish of movement in her belly, not quite a kick yet, but a definite presence with a determined opinion, continued. The shifting pressure settled right onto her bladder again. With her hand on her belly, and tears threatening the corners of her eyes, Josie squeezed her thighs together and whispered a plea. "Please quiet down, Junior. I'm trying to make an exit here."

WITH FOURTH PRECINCT Chief Mitch Taylor running the Monday morning roll call meeting, Rafe was doing his best to pay attention. But the vivid memories of Josie's touch on his skin, her hand cradling his seed in her belly and the battleground of emotions waging war inside him made it a real challenge.

"I want to remind everybody about the spring carnival we're putting together for the KCPD widows and orphans fund this month." Mitch Taylor pulled back the front of his jacket and propped his hands at his waist in a stance that indicated this project was every bit as important to him as the ongoing investigations on his agenda. His booming voice required no microphone. "Mark your calendars for Memorial Day weekend. Even though we've hired an event planner to coordinate the event, I'll be looking for volunteers to help with everything from parking to running the arcade games for the kids."

Rafe would make sure he didn't get on the fun and games list, although he had every intention of helping. Besides being a successful fundraiser for a worthy cause, he wanted to be a part of the annual event that honored his fallen comrades, including his first partner, Aaron Nichols, and Dominic Molloy, a member of his original SWAT team who had been killed in the line of duty a couple of years earlier. Rafe understood the unspoken command in Chief Taylor's request for volunteers, and had every intention of complying.

But as he leaned against the back counter between his commanding officer, Captain Michael Cutler, and the rookie on the team, sharpshooter Miranda Murdock, his focus wandered. While the chief moved on to updates about ongoing cases, Be On the Lookout for suspects, or BOLOs, and other points of concern, Rafe swept his gaze across the detectives and uniformed officers crowding into the fourth floor conference room.

This, he understood. Requests from the precinct chief. Morning reports. Strong coffee burning his tongue. The Glock 9 mm strapped to his thigh.

Lists. Rules. Expectations. He trained hard to be a SWAT cop, did his damnedest to be worthy of the trust he shared with his team. He obeyed orders and gave them with equal alacrity. He knew the penalties for failing to do his job—a reprimand, a demotion, a bullet.

So he could care about his work. He could invest himself in being a career cop because he understood his job inside and out.

What he didn't understand were people and the unpredictability of their emotions. Why had Calvin Chambers's murder hit him so hard? It wasn't the first death he'd had to deal with on the job. He'd lost things far more personal than a boy he'd only known for the ten minutes he'd bled out in his arms. Why had dumping his raw emotions on Josie Nichols, pouring himself into her willing body and loving arms felt like the only balm that could assuage the grief and anger he'd felt that night? Where had that need come from?

He'd betrayed a promise to Aaron Nichols. He'd taken advantage of a friendship and that crazy, flattering, foolish crush Josie had always had on him. He'd given in to the simmering male awareness of her long legs and silky hair that he'd studiously ignored for ages because he knew damn well that he wasn't marriage material. Josie could do better than him. She deserved a happily-ever-after that no moody, brooding bastard like him could ever give her.

He liked the black-and-white assurance of routine and regulations. He hated the gray area of relationships. If a child loved his parents, and trusted that they loved him in return, then why use him as a whipping post to vent their frustrations with the world? If a young man wanted to be worthy of the faith of a mentor, then why promise to take care of a family when he lacked the skills to do so?

If a beautiful young woman told him he was going to be a father, then why couldn't he feel joy? Why couldn't he see the result of a night of feral compassion as anything other than a huge mistake for both of them?

Where were the rules he could apply to relationships? He understood the anger she'd directed toward him Friday night. He'd been even more angry at himself for putting her into this situation. So why did it stick in his craw that Josie had kept her pregnancy a secret from him?

"I don't want anything from you. Just think of this baby as all mine. I do."

He wasn't sure if it was hurt or anger or maybe even

shame that she hadn't trusted him enough to tell him the news. So maybe he had been a particularly moody son of a gun lately—a child's senseless death did that to a man. But that night in his truck had been, what, six months ago? Hell of a long time to keep a secret.

He'd never intended to be a father, but hadn't ten years of looking out for her taught her that he'd do the right thing by her and the baby? She'd rejected his offer to take care of her outright less than an hour ago. She'd rejected his brotherly advice about the Kyle Austin murder. She'd walked away as though she didn't want a damn thing from him if she couldn't have everything. And he couldn't, he just couldn't, open up like that again.

But she didn't need to be working on her feet every spare hour she wasn't sleeping or studying. She didn't need to be dealing with Patrick and prison visitations and trying to save the lives of convicted kidnappers.

Whatever he was feeling didn't matter. Keeping his promise to Aaron Nichols demanded that Rafe do something about Josie and her baby. Despite her protests, he could pay her bills, start some kind of insurance or trust fund for the kid. He'd take more responsibility with Patrick, too. Hell, getting him off the streets and into jail and its mandatory drug rehab program had probably saved Patrick's life, although Rafe was sure Josie's half brother didn't see it that way.

Rafe stared down into the coffee mug he held in his hand, thinking the rich, dark color didn't do justice to Josie's glorious hair. He remembered what the long, velvety softness had felt like clutched between his fingers, what its citrusy scent had smelled like filling up his senses.

And just as that forbidden desire stirred in his veins, he saw the hand gripping the mug and a grim observation hit him like a punch to the gut. The scars that marked his fingers and knuckles were just the tangible evidence of what Josie must see when she looked at him. He was beat up, inside and out. The marks from his childhood ran deep. The detachment he needed to do the work he did had been polished and reinforced like a well-fitted suit of body armor. He was tough, intensely private and on guard against the world 24/7. He certainly wasn't the patient, warm kind of fuzzy that a child needed or a woman might want for the long haul.

He needed rules and predictability and black-and-white.

A young mother needed patience and flexibility and lots of sympathetic support—things that just weren't in him to give.

Josie had been smart to keep the baby's existence from him. It was a matter of self-preservation. An emotional survival tactic.

And *that* was something Rafe understood in spades.

Didn't mean he was going to let her shoulder the responsibilities of parenthood all by herself. He'd find a way to ease her burden somehow.

"Sarge." Captain Cutler's whisper nudged Rafe from his thoughts. "Late night?"

Rafe slowly shifted on his feet, quickly scanning his surroundings and calculating just how many seconds had passed since he'd been aware of the meeting. "What?"

"You're miles away from here." The captain pointed to the half-empty mug Rafe held, then to the front of the room. "Drink your coffee and pay attention."

Chief Taylor's gaze went to the back of the room where they stood, his sharp eyes meeting Rafe's for a moment, sending a silent message that seemed to say *"Welcome back to my world, Sarge."*

"...put our SWAT teams and bomb squads on alert," Chief Taylor said, his watchful eyes moving on to the next target who might not be completely focused on the details of the morning report. "These may be random, isolated threats against Quinn Gallagher. But the flak vests that most of you are wearing were probably made by Gallagher's company, so a little reciprocal protection has been approved by the commissioner."

"What kind of protection are we talking about, Mitch?" Captain Cutler asked.

The chief inhaled a deep breath that expanded his barrel-size chest. "Obviously, we can't favor one citizen of Kansas City over another, so if you're on a call, that takes priority. Just be prepared to do a thorough walk-through of Gallagher headquarters or any of the company's plants in the area if another threat is received. And it couldn't hurt to familiarize your team with the security setup Gallagher has in place around his home and workplaces in case we need to make an incursion there."

"Will do."

Rafe knew that Michael Cutler and mega-wiz security billionaire Quinn Gallagher had been friends for several years, so he had a feeling that a simple "walk-through" wouldn't be good enough if another threat was made. He'd better prep the rest of the team to expect some extra demands on their time if they got called out on a situation with Gallagher Security Systems.

"And while we're on the subject of SWAT," Chief Taylor continued, his stern countenance actually dredging up a smile for the man towering on the other side of Miranda Murdock. "I want to welcome back Trip Jones to SWAT Team One. After a stint in the hospital, rehab and—did I hear a honeymoon?—he finally decided to show up for work today. He may have a couple more holes in him—but it's good to see him standing tall and taking up just as much space as he did before the shooting."

Trip nodded. "Thank you, sir."

A burst of applause filled the room and everyone seated at the tables turned to face the five uniformed men in black standing at the back of the room.

A few months earlier, Trip had gone head to head with a speeding van and three armed perps to save the woman he loved. Rafe and the rest of the team had arrived on the scene to help put away the trio of would-be kidnappers, but not before Trip had nearly died in the confrontation. Rafe counted on one hand the number of men he called friend. It was good to have one of those rare ones back on the team.

As the applause and good wishes were dying down, Rafe reached in front of Murdock to butt fists with the man towering on the other side of her. "Good to see you in one piece, big guy."

With a grin, Trip touched fists. "Good to be in one."

For a few seconds, Rafe was smiling, too. He was relaxed and firmly back into cop mode where he felt most comfortable.

For a few seconds.

The last item on Chief Taylor's agenda dragged Rafe back out of his comfort zone. "Now I'm turning the meeting over to Detective Montgomery so he can update us on where we stand with the Rich Girl Killer. Spencer?"

Rafe pulled away from the counter where he'd been leaning and stood squarely on his feet as the red-haired detective in the fancy suit and tie walked up to the podium at the front of the room and opened a notebook. Spencer Montgomery was the detective who'd grilled Josie about the prisoner she'd tried to save at the prison visitation center. Trip and the fifth member of their team, the chief's nephew, Alex Taylor, perked up, as well. Both had had run-ins with the tenacious Mr. Montgomery over his investigation into the Rich Girl Murders.

SWAT Team One's almost adversarial scrutiny wasn't lost on Detective Montgomery, but it was dismissed with a nod before he calmly adjusted his tie and addressed the entire room. "My partner, Nick, is distributing images of the man we believe to be the RGK or Rich Girl Killer. The small picture is what he looked like ten years ago."

Rafe's attention briefly shifted to the short, stocky man handing out copies of a computer printout. The nondescript high-school yearbook photo he gave him could have belonged to any pimply-faced teen with glasses. As soon as Rafe had gotten a glimpse of the generic drawing of a man with a bad toupee in his hands, his gaze went back to Montgomery, silently daring him to justify his reasons for questioning Josie at all. The RGK targeted wealthy women, not working-class angels like Josie Nichols. She didn't need to be involved in his investigation.

But Montgomery was nothing if not cool, calm and able to dismiss any challenge to his expertise. "We have every reason to believe that the RGK is responsible for the recent murder of Kyle Austin at the detention center. Austin admitted to copying the RGK's tactics when he attempted to kidnap and murder his stepsister, Charlotte Mayweather, and her testimony corroborates that." Rafe glanced over at Trip. Normally, the most easygoing of the team, he stood with his arms crossed and his shoulders puffed up in disapproval of Montgomery mentioning his new wife's name. "Miss Mayweather—pardon me, the new Mrs. Jones—gave us our strongest lead in the case. She suspects—and I concur—that the RGK is Donald Rathbone Kemp, someone she and the other victims once went to school with. However, based on an eyewitness description of Austin's killer, she could not identify this man as the boy she once knew in high school."

Eyewitness description? Ah, hell. Josie was in this up to her eyeballs.

"So your witness's description of the RGK is pretty worthless, yes?" a detective at a table near the front of the room asked.

Rafe bristled at the unintended slur against Josie. Not that she apparently thought it was any of his business to know just how involved she was in Montgomery's case.

"Quite the contrary," Montgomery countered. "There's no record of a Donald Kemp in the system, so we believe that he's assumed a new identity or possibly has access to several identities. We also believe that he's had plastic surgery to alter his appearance and/or is a master at disguising himself. Chief Taylor wants us to be vigilant about spotting this man when you're walking your beat or answering other calls. I want to put him in a lineup and see if our witness can identify him."

A uniformed officer groused from the far side of the room. "Do you expect us to stop every man on the street and compare him to this drawing?"

"I can narrow down the profile for you," Montgomery answered. "We're looking for a very clever man— someone who takes pride in his intelligence or expertise in whatever job he's currently pursuing."

"He feels superior to those around him," his partner, Nick Fensom, added, "even if he's working in a menial position. And, as we know from the victims he chooses, he'll resent those in positions of power or authority over him."

Montgomery turned a page in his notebook. "Based on the crime scenes we've studied, we know that he also suffers from obsessive-compulsive disorder. So we're looking for someone who is fastidious about his appcarance and will surround himself with a clean, tidy environment, whether it be the bus he's driving or the briefcase he carries with him to work. If it's soiled or out of place, it'll bother this guy."

Rafe took note of every detail, thinking the description sounded a little too familiar, considering he'd grown up with a father who, if his drinking hadn't killed him four years ago, could be a viable suspect. And Josie had gotten close to this guy? His irritation with Detective Montgomery waned as he imagined a man like his violent father going anywhere near Josie or her baby. A tight fist of protective anger squeezed in his gut.

And then Montgomery's partner joined him at the podium and listed a trio of Kemp's relatives—a father and two uncles who were serving time in prison for the kidnapping of Trip's wife back when she was a teenager. "They were professional grifters, nomads who apparently taught Kemp from the time he was a boy to take part in whatever con they were staging. Failure, according to his uncle, was met with a beating, which sets up our unsub's penchant for violence. When KCPD arrested the father and uncles nine years ago, there was no sign of Kemp. Speculation was that he might have been killed because he failed at his role in the kidnapping. But we no longer believe that's the case. Instead, he went off the radar and assumed a new identity."

"His family—these uncles and father—haven't provided any help in locating Kemp?" Chief Taylor asked.

Nick Fensom shook his head. "They haven't seen or heard from him since before their arrests. They each said they thought Donny was dead."

"Or so they claim," the chief scoffed. "You did say they were con men. How do we know this guy is still in Kansas City?"

Detective Montgomery closed his notebook and made a grim pronouncement. "Because he doesn't like loose ends, sir. He was trained to clean up any mistake.

A witness saw him commit murder, saw a version of his adult face. He won't leave the area until he silences that witness."

Enough profiling mumbo-jumbo. If Montgomery was right, then it was only a matter of time before the RGK went looking for Josie. "Do you have plans to put that witness in a safe house?"

To his credit, Spencer Montgomery didn't seem surprised that Rafe had just stuck his nose into what was typically a matter for detectives and uniforms who interacted with the public on a more regular basis than SWAT cops. "That witness is anonymous, and will remain so until we have a man in custody and a positive identification has been made." He turned and nodded to Chief Taylor. "That's our report, sir."

"All right then, ladies and gentlemen—let's find this guy." The rustle of notepads closing and papers being tucked away indicated the end of the morning briefing, but no one moved from their seat until Mitch Taylor gave the word. "Watch your backs out there. Dismissed."

Rafe pushed his way through the exodus filing from the conference room, zeroing in on the shock of red hair moving into the hallway ahead of him. "Montgomery!" He excused himself past a pair of chatty detectives and caught up to him. "I want to talk to you."

Signaling his partner to go ahead, Montgomery turned from the flow of traffic toward the main room's maze of cubicles and stepped aside to get a drink of water from the nearby fountain before he answered. "I'm aware you have a personal connection to my investigation, Sergeant Delgado." He straightened to face

Rafe. "Ironic, isn't it, that two of the RGK's intended victims have wound up under the personal protection of SWAT Team One. An outside observer might think your team is interfering with my investigation."

Rafe wasn't interested in irony or explaining that Montgomery might be investigating two more deaths instead of attempted murders if members of his team hadn't stepped up to keep those targeted women safe. "You need to set up some kind of protection for Josie Nichols. Did she even agree to this? It's a damn stupid strategy to publicly announce that she's seen the Rich Girl Killer."

Montgomery leaned forward and hushed his voice. "Am I the one who just said her name out loud? And yes, she agreed to look at a lineup for me. She's like her dad in that regard—not afraid to do her public duty."

"Are you sure you explained the risk she was taking? That you didn't con her into identifying a serial killer? That profile you gave could be you, you arrogant son of—" Rafe raked his fingers through his short hair, taking a breath while another officer walked past. Then he dropped his voice to match the detective's terse whisper. "You care more about your case than any collateral damage you may cause. She's vulnerable to that bastard, and you know it."

"She's the safest woman in Kansas City, if you ask me." The detective's light-colored eyes looked dead serious. He gestured toward Rafe. "Everywhere she turns, she's surrounded by cops. Big brother. At the Shamrock. All those friends of her father's. What killer is going to risk approaching her?"

"What about when she's at home? Alone."

"Like I said…she remains completely anonymous. Hidden in plain sight." He shrugged and buttoned the front of his suit jacket. "Unless you slip and tell someone her name, like you did just now. I know I won't."

Rafe burned inside, warring with the need to throttle some sense into Josie—seemingly out to singlehandedly save Kansas City from a serial killer when she should be concentrating on taking care of herself and the baby—and simply wanting to throttle Spencer here for taking advantage of her willingness to help anyone and everyone in need. "I don't like you, Montgomery."

"Well, I won't lose any sleep over that. And it won't keep me from doing my job." Nick Fensom came back to the conference room area and gave his partner a high sign, indicating the time. "Now if you'll excuse me, I have a press briefing to get to downstairs. The sooner we ID Kemp in his current alias and get him off the streets, the sooner my witness will be safe."

His witness.

As if Josie belonged to him.

Josie and the baby belonged to…well… They sure as hell didn't belong to Spencer Montgomery. And they weren't pawns Rafe was willing to risk, even if it meant catching a killer. Rafe inhaled a deep breath, then ran a palmful of water from the fountain and splashed it against his cheeks and the back of his neck, needing to cool his jets and think this thing through.

Aaron would be rolling over in his grave if he knew about the potential danger an unlucky meeting in a prison visitation room had put Josie in. Rafe ran his damp fingers over the top of his hair, smoothing the mess he'd made earlier. He had to do something.

Fensom and Montgomery were long gone, and the conference room nearly cleared out, by the time Rafe had reached his decision. Josie would hate him for what he was going to propose. He made a wry sound that wasn't quite a laugh. Like he wasn't on her hit list already.

"Sarge?"

He heard Captain Cutler's voice behind him, along with several congratulatory comments from coworkers welcoming Trip back after his medical leave. With just a nod, Rafe turned and joined the rest of the five-man team as they crossed past the detectives' stations and sergeant's desk on their way to the bank of elevators that would take them down to the garage level where the SWAT teams were based.

Keep her identity secret. He couldn't even tell his team that Josie Nichols was Montgomery's star witness—the one person who'd seen the RGK's current face. He couldn't risk her name slipping out in connection to the case, even accidentally.

But silence and a scowl couldn't go undetected by a man as observant as Michael Cutler for long. He pushed the elevator's call button, crossed his arms in front of him and asked, "So what's eating you this morning?" While the others gathered out of earshot behind them, Cutler angled his dark blue eyes toward Rafe. "Anything I can help with?"

Michael was too good a friend to lie to him outright. And he was too smart to believe any denial Rafe could come up with. So a half truth would have to suffice. Something was bothering him. Big time. "Josie's pregnant."

He turned his head to face him, although any initial surprise or pleasure at the news quickly slipped behind an objective mask. "I take it you're not pleased. Between school and all the jobs she holds down, I didn't know she had time for a relationship."

"She doesn't."

"So this wasn't planned."

"No."

"Is the father in the picture?" Rafe stared straight ahead. "I'm guessing she's having to practically hog-tie you to keep you from coming down hard on the guy."

Rafe glanced his way for a moment, sending a mute distress message.

The captain could be counted on to be perceptive. This time, he didn't hide his surprise. "I didn't know you and… Well, it's about time. I mean, you and Josie were the only two people who never seemed to see the sparks between—"

"We're not a couple."

Right. This isn't good news. The message registered clear on Cutler's expression. "But you are the father?"

"I don't do relationships. We're just…friends. That's all we've ever been." Rafe wheeled around to face his captain straight-on. "Can you see me as a dad? Don't answer that."

Captain Cutler's eyes narrowed. Ah, hell. He was the team's negotiator, trained to read the slightest nuances about people—and Rafe had just revealed a lot more than a nuance about his unfamiliar, conflicted emotions. "Do we need to talk about this?"

"No."

"Because I've got some experience with fatherhood.

It's just as scary as you think, yet it's the best job in the world. I'm surviving the teenage years with Mike and there's another one on the way. The pregnancy routine with the doctor and prenatal classes have changed a little bit since Mike was born. But the basics are the same. If you have questions…"

Michael Cutler was exactly the kind of man who should be a father. Patient teacher. Good listener. Strong leader. Proud. Loyal. Rafe didn't need that kind of pressure to try to live up to and fall short. A bell dinged and he turned to face the elevator again. "I'm good."

"All right. The offer stands if and when you're ready to talk. Meanwhile, we've got a lot on our plate right now with the Gallagher Security threats and the RGK on the loose. I need you to focus. Can you do your job today?"

Rafe knew it was a serious question. He gave Michael a serious answer. "Always. That's one thing you can always count on, sir."

The elevator doors opened and they stepped inside. "Then let's check the gear and be ready to roll."

Chapter Four

Crossing through the lobby of Fourth Precinct head-quarters proved to be no easy task.

The clicks and flashes of cameras, and hushed buzz of reporters speaking into cell phones and microphones, vaguely reminded Rafe of the barrage of gunfire and flash bangs the team had used to neutralize a hypothetical terrorist threat on their last run through the KCPD training facility. Not exactly a good omen for the outcome of Spencer Montgomery's press conference.

All five members of SWAT Team One slowed their steps to negotiate their way through the crowd gathering around the podium where Chief Taylor was making introductions. But it was Trip, with his wry sense of humor, who said exactly what Rafe had been thinking. "I knew we were fighting a war on crime, but, in our own lobby?"

"They want answers like everyone else in Kansas City," Miranda suggested. "It's been two years since the Rich Girl Killer first got a name. It was an isolated murder when Quinn Gallagher's wife was killed. As soon as he struck again, he became a serial killer and the wealthy families of Kansas City went on alert. Big money and big news go together."

She was onto something there. Rafe's hands fisted at his sides. These reporters were a lot more interested in covering a break in a case where the city's elite were targeted than, say, the murder of a working-class schoolboy who'd been shot walking home from school and had died in a police officer's arms.

All the more reason to keep Josie's name out of the investigation. Not only would the extra publicity make it nearly impossible to keep her a Jane Doe, but the notoriety would thrust her into a spotlight that nobody in their right mind would want to be a part of.

Rafe fixed his gaze on Spencer Montgomery as he thanked Chief Taylor and stepped up to the microphone. He'd better damn well be true to his word and keep any mention or description of Josie out of his presentation.

"Could you hurry up?" A shrill man's voice from near the front door couldn't shake Rafe's focus. "I've got a living to make here. Today?"

Since Montgomery was getting the room up to speed on the investigation details to date, and hadn't even held up Josie's description of the killer yet, Rafe turned to see what the commotion behind him was about. He saw a balding linebacker of a reporter grab his camera from the security guard who'd cleared him through the front door checkpoint and barrel toward him. Rafe tried to step aside, but the man was intent on looping the camera strap around his neck and the collision was inevitable.

"Whoa. Sorry, officer, uh…" The stout man angled his head to read Rafe's name off his uniform pocket. "…Delgado. Excuse me."

Rafe's eyes narrowed as recognition tried to kick in. "Don't I know you?"

Trip had moved to block the man's path. With his arms crossed over his chest like that, the big guy made an effective roadblock. "His name's Steve Lassen."

There was a name that rang an unpleasant bell. Lassen had once been a respected reporter for the *Kansas City Journal,* but a rumored drinking problem and a taste for the money that more sensationalistic stories could bring in had turned him into nothing better than a tabloid hound whose reporter's "instincts" had even jeopardized a couple of KCPD cases.

Alex Taylor closed the triangle around the reporter, preventing him from moving on. "What are you doing here, Lassen?" Alex taunted. "This press conference is for legitimate reporters. I'm surprised they let you in the door."

Lassen smoothed his graying, blond-brown hair into place and turned to Alex. "I got my press pass back, Taylor, no thanks to you." He tilted his gaze to include Trip in his sneering explanation, as well. "I've been following the progress of this Rich Girl Killer. I've even scooped my colleagues with a few select quotes and photos of some of the players involved in the investigation."

Alex inched forward, stopping just shy of invading the tabloid reporter's personal space. "You only scooped the competition because you were contaminating crime scenes before they'd been cordoned off and were harassing potential witnesses."

Lassen held his hands up as if he was daring to be arrested. "You'll be pleased to know I no longer have any interest in your fiancée, Ms. Kline. Unless, of course, as a member of the District Attorney's office, the Rich

Girl Killer case lands on her desk. But I'm guessing his capture will be big enough news in Kansas City that the D.A. himself will handle the case."

"Gentlemen." Captain Cutler's authoritative voice intervened. "We have no reason to detain Mr. Lassen."

"Ah, a voice of reason." Lassen's smirk turned into a smile as Cutler's order drew his attention beyond Trip and Alex. "If you fine gentlemen—and beautiful young lady—will excuse me." He pulled a business card from his pocket and turned his full attention to Miranda. "Maybe you and I could get together sometime and talk about what it's like for a woman like you to wear so much body armor. But later. I don't want to miss a single detail of what Detective Montgomery has to say about the investigation. Word on the street is he's got a surviving witness who can identify the RGK."

"A woman like me? What did he mean by that?" That's right. Set Randy Murdock off with some comment that hinted she was too blonde and too pretty to be a SWAT cop. Then the rest of them could stand back and let her cut Lassen off at the knees.

"Easy, Murdock," Cutler warned as she crunched the business card in her fist. He motioned Trip and Alex to stand aside and let Lassen join the press conference. "He's practicing his Constitutional right to be a jackass."

"Montgomery's witness won't survive for long if Lassen scoops her identity." Rafe avoided saying Josie's name, but he had to put it out there. "Even if he just speculates on who the witness might be, he could be signing a death warrant. Maybe he'll do the right thing and just print the composite photo Montgomery handed out. Only put people on the lookout for Donny Kemp, or whoever he is now."

"He won't do the right thing," Alex said. "That guy makes my blood boil. I hate him even saying Audrey's name."

"How do you think he's *scooping* anyone else on Montgomery's investigation?" Trip asked.

Alex had an answer that made them both snicker. "Because he hangs out with the same lowlife devil scum as the RGK."

The captain's cell phone rang, and Rafe's vibrated on his belt. One by one they all were being summoned. The entire team's attention shifted from Lassen and Montgomery to the details they could pick up from Michael Cutler's side of the phone call.

By the time Cutler hung up, they were already half briefed. "Show's over for us, guys. We've got a domestic disturbance over on Paseo with reports of a gun on the premises. We need to move out."

"Yes, sir." Rafe, Trip, Alex and Randy answered in unison. As the other three jogged to the stairwell leading down to the garage where the SWAT van was parked, Rafe spared another moment to scan Detective Montgomery's smooth facade and gauge the reaction of the reporters as they viewed the computerized image of the RGK being flashed up on the viewscreen.

"Sergeant." The captain's voice commanded action. "You're driving. Let's move."

With a nod, Rafe backed away from the chaos and followed the captain to the stairs. But he stopped and turned one last time to get a good look at the heavyset reporter with the receding points in his hairline. It took only a second to imprint Steve Lassen's face and build in his memory, and then Rafe was jogging down the stairs, taking them three at a time to catch up with the others.

Lassen had terrorized Alex Taylor's fiancée, an assistant district attorney, opting for an exposé on her personal life instead of doing some serious reporting about the gang leader she'd convicted for murdering Calvin Chambers. Then Lassen had moved on to heiress Charlotte Mayweather, the wealthy recluse who'd barely survived a kidnapping as a teenager. When she'd come out of hiding to pay her respects to a close family friend who'd been slain trying to protect her, Lassen had been at the cemetery to catch the grieving woman on camera. Trip had rescued Charlotte that day—and wound up marrying her. But not before the RGK had come close to killing them, too.

Steve Lassen was a magnet for trouble. And the *low-life devil scum* as Alex had so eloquently put it, was something even more dangerous.

If Lassen came within a mile of Josie, Rafe would recognize him on sight. And if he showed any hint that he knew *she* was Montgomery's anonymous witness, Rafe would see to it personally that Lassen's reporting days were over.

"GREAT WORK." JOSIE's supervising R.N., Julia Taylor, signed off at the bottom of the screen where she'd scanned each of the supplies in this bay of the Truman Medical Center's emergency room. "I'll add these to my requisition list."

As the friendly trauma nurse closed down one

computer file and pulled up another, Josie succumbed to the length of the day, rolling her shoulders forward and twisting to reach the muscle knotting in the small of her back. But a soft moan gave her away.

"Unfortunately, nursing seems to be as much about paperwork as it is…" Julia stood up from the stool where she'd been sitting and rolled it across the floor toward Josie. "How long have you been on your feet today? Sit."

Josie hesitated, not wanting to give any indication that she wasn't fit for this job she'd been training so long and hard for.

"Sit," Julia ordered, her easy smile softening any hint of a reprimand. "I think I was in my third month with MacKinley when the twinge in my lower back started. It lasted right through to the second week past her due date when we finally had to induce her. Thank goodness my husband knows how to give a good massage."

A massage from a loving husband. She wished. Josie had been settling for hot showers and strategically placed pillows to give her swelling body some relief at night. She willingly sank onto the cushioned seat, splaying her hands over her belly and smoothing her loose green top over the telltale baby bump. "Is it that obvious I'm pregnant?"

Julia arched a dark blond eyebrow into a skeptical frown. "Is it supposed to be a secret?" Before Josie could answer, her supervisor pulled the curtain separating this trauma bay from the one beside it to give them a little more privacy. Then she propped her hands on her ample hips and faced her. "You've got the height and build to carry the baby without showing too much.

But you're what, five, six months along?" She pulled up another stool and sat beside her. "I don't think even loose lab jackets and extra-large scrubs can hide the baby anymore. And believe me, around here, you don't have to. I think it's a sign of strength to do meaningful work while you're pregnant. It certainly takes your mind off some of the aches and awkwardness you're going through."

In a way, Josie was glad that Julia had seen through her recent penchant for baggy clothing. The long breath that eased from her chest sounded a lot like a sigh of relief. "How long have you known?"

"Well, since I've helped with several deliveries here and I've given birth to two of my own, I was pretty certain when you started your E.R. rotation a couple of months ago. I assumed you'd share the news when you were ready to."

"I didn't want it to interfere with my work here. Trauma nursing is where I want to specialize, and I wanted to make sure I got a good report. I don't want any special considerations."

"Please." Julia practically snorted. "Your grades are top notch, you're great with the patients and you absorb everything you see or hear. Needing a few minutes here and there to take care of yourself won't keep you from getting a good report from me." Her tone changed to the calm efficiency she used with the sick and injured who came through the E.R. "Is everything going as it should with you and the baby?"

"Yes. We're both perfectly healthy." Josie named the nurse midwife she was seeing and listed the supplements she was taking.

"She's good." Julia rolled her stool a few inches closer. "So, do you know the sex? Have you picked out names?"

Josie shared a laugh and truly relaxed for the first time since breaking the news of her pregnancy to Rafe. It felt wonderfully decadent to trade some normal conversation about the baby with a friend who saw the life growing inside her as a good thing. "I want the gender to be a surprise when he or she is born. And I'm thinking of old family names. Aaron for my dad if it's a boy, and Aileen for my grandmother if it's a girl."

Julia's gaze dropped to the suspiciously unadorned fingers on Josie's left hand. "And can I be shamefully inappropriate and ask about the daddy?"

Even though her smile faded, Josie found the older woman's compassionate curiosity made it possible to talk about Rafe. "He's a cop at KCPD. A good man. He used to be my dad's partner before he died. We've been friends forever and we kind of forgot that once and…" Josie knit her fingers together over the butterfly tremors she felt moving inside her. "Now it's hard to even be friends sometimes."

"Anyone I know?" Julia asked. "With Taylor for a last name, it feels like I'm related to half the cops on KCPD anymore."

"I'd rather not say."

Julie nodded her understanding at Josie's desire to keep at least that one piece of information private. "Does he know about the baby?"

"I told him last week. Or rather, it slipped out during an argument. Not my finest moment." Her heart twisted with a familiar pain. Rafe had only been trying to help and she'd thrown the news of the baby at him like some kind of accusation. "I guess I was hoping that we could work things out between us before I told him. But I'm resigning myself to the fact that if *us* is never going to happen, then he's not interested in being a father to my baby, either."

"If he's a good man like you say, he'll come around. Give him a chance to do the right thing." Reaching across the space between them, Julia gently squeezed Josie's hand. "You've had six months to get used to the idea of starting a family—he's only had a few days."

"I suppose." Although Josie wasn't sure she had the strength to keep hoping that Rafe would ever give himself permission to see where a relationship between them would go, she appreciated Julia's kind words. "I just have to be patient, hmm?"

"It's a mother's lot in life." The other nurse pulled away and picked up the electronic computer pad. "While you're waiting, I'll try to keep you busy. You can finish taking inventory of the last two trauma bays."

Josie stood when she did. "Yes, ma'am."

"It's Julia, please." Her supervisor held on to the pad when Josie reached for it. "If you need a break, take it. As long as we're not in the middle of dealing with a patient, of course. And if you have any questions related to your schooling, or to your little one there, we can talk. I'm a pretty good listener."

"Thanks, Julia."

Although her back didn't ache any less, Josie's spirits lifted a little as she continued her work. Her conversation with Julia Taylor had eased the funk she'd been in for the past few days, if not the worries about single parenthood, a surly papa-to-be or the premeditated murder of a man in prison. Her baby's safety and well-being came first. If she could help Spencer Montgomery with his investigation, she would, just as long as he kept her name, and thus the baby's existence, out of the spotlight.

As for everything else? Rafe? Graduation? Happiness? Success? Love? That's what the future was for. Right now, she only had the strength to worry about today.

Two hours, one motorcycle accident with a broken arm and wounds the doctor had Josie debride or stitch up, and a completed inventory later, and she was hurrying across the employee parking lot.

She barely had time to go back to her apartment to change into some jeans and grab a sandwich before heading over to the Shamrock. Not that Uncle Robbie ever gave her grief if she was late for her shift, but he relied on her to keep things running smoothly at the bar, probably more than he realized.

As she saw the beginnings of rush-hour traffic lining up on the main road east of the hospital, she cradled her tummy and broke into a jog, weaving through row after row of parked cars until she reached her Fiesta. She unlocked the door and tossed her backpack onto the passenger seat as she slid in behind the wheel. She inserted her key and reached for her seat belt. But when she tried to start the engine, nothing. Just clicks and silence.

"Not now," she groused. She ran her gaze over the dashboard. Gas, good. Temperature, normal. The oil thingee, where it was supposed to be. Josie took a deep breath, turned the key.

"Oh, no. No, no, no." She held her mouth just right and tried one more time. *Click. Click. Click.* "Damn it!" She pounded her fist on the steering wheel in frustration, then just as quickly caressed her stomach. "Don't you say words like that, little one. Mommy's mad and a little tired. You should try to remain calm and fix your problem, rather than just swearing at it." With a glance at her watch and a shake of her head, she popped the hood and climbed out of the car, heeding her own advice.

Not that she knew what she was looking at once she'd propped the hood open. She could put air in her tires and add washer fluid, but even this miniature engine mocked her like a puzzle she couldn't decipher. Still, she pulled back the loose ends of her lab jacket, and reached in to pull out the oil-level indicator and jiggle a hose. Even if she knew what she was looking for, she didn't have the tools to fix it.

Squashing down the urge to curse again, she pulled her phone from her pocket. Who was she supposed to call for something like this? Six months ago, without hesitation, she'd have dialed Rafe Delgado. But with that relationship now in a shambles, she was left with either Uncle Robbie, who would be in the middle of setup for the evening crowd at the Shamrock—or the unplanned costs of a tow truck and repair bill.

Josie was silently bemoaning the delay and resigning herself to pulling Uncle Robbie from work when a man came around the car next to hers and spoke. "Having problems with your car?"

Josie reeled from the man who seemed to have materialized from thin air, instinctively clutching her heart and her belly.

He stopped in his tracks, held up both hands in an apologetic gesture and smiled. "Sorry, I didn't mean to startle you."

"It's me." She calmed her nerves and summoned up a smile herself. "I'm running late and feeling a little stressed."

He moved up beside her to peek beneath the hood. "Isn't that the way? Mechanical things always wait until the worst possible moment to break down."

"I guess." Her heart rate returned to a normal rhythm as he adjusted the bill of the black baseball cap he wore and bent over the engine to inspect it. "It makes a clicking noise when I turn the key."

The man wore light blue scrubs, indicating he was surgical staff. And even though she didn't recognize the buzz cut of hair or remember a San Francisco Giants fan from her rotation in the surgery wing, Josie knew the medical center had hundreds of people on staff, and even more consultants and medical students like herself who came and went throughout the year. Maybe he was military, she thought, noting the plain black glasses he adjusted at his temple, someone who'd been deployed and had recently returned. She couldn't be expected to know everyone on staff, could she?

"Are you new here?" she asked, hoping he'd either introduce himself or make some kind of connection that wouldn't make him seem like such a mysterious stranger. "Maybe you know Rae Sams? She's in my class at UMKC. She's working in the SICU now."

"I'm new." But no name. No acknowledgment of her friend.

Awkward.

"I'm Josie," she offered, stepping around the fender out of his way as he scooted over to reach something behind the battery. "Do you know a lot about cars?"

His hand, scrubbed clean as if prepped for surgery, despite tinkering with her engine, slid toward the spot where hers rested on the frame of the car, stopping just shy of touching her. "A woman alone should be more careful about taking care of her things, Josie."

A woman alone? Josie snatched her hand away. Was he hitting on her? Or was she reading a threat into his words that wasn't there? She hugged her arms around the baby and retreated a step, her hips butting up against the car behind her. The feeling of being suddenly trapped made her pulse leap. "Look, I appreciate the help, but maybe I better just call—"

"When are you due?" He straightened from beneath the hood, glancing her way beneath the brim of his cap without directly facing her. "Babies are such precious things, aren't they?"

"In August. I, um…" Take better care of her things? *Precious things?* The May afternoon was still sunny, yet she found herself rubbing at an unexpected prickle of goose bumps along her arms. "Who are you?"

She tried to get a better angle to read the name tag hanging from his chest pocket. Shifting in her white clogs, she was torn between the need to look him straight in the eye to get some answers and the urge to run.

Heavy tires braking on the pavement and the slam

of a truck door diverted her attention for a split second. "Josie?" a deep voice called.

Her breath rushed out at the crunch of booted feet. "Rafe?"

He circled the hood of his truck, striding toward her. "What's wrong with that rattletrap now?"

He froze at the touch of her fingers brushing over the center buttons of his black uniform shirt. She savored the familiar sensations of starched cotton and stiff Kevlar, and the warmth emanating from the skin beneath. Instead of asking why he'd shown up at the hospital when he was probably still on the clock, she curled her fingers into her palm and gave him the space his wary posture seemed to ask for. Having him here with that weirdo checking her car was good enough. She tipped her chin to meet the question in his dark eyes. "I'm glad you're here. My car worked fine this morning, but now it won't start. And he…"

She turned around, but the creepy good Samaritan was gone.

Josie dashed to the front of the car. "Where did he go?"

"Who?"

"There was a man." She jerked her head to the right, then the left. Building. Cars. Pedestrians. Trees. But no man in a black ball cap and surgical blue scrubs. A nervous breath caught in her chest. She looked again.

She heard Rafe walk up behind her. "What's going on? You're freaking me out a little bit."

Join the club.

Josie turned. She curled her fingertips beneath the placket of his shirt and pulled herself into the broad shelter of his chest. "Don't argue with me for two seconds, okay?" she begged, shivering in the late-day sunshine. "Just hold me."

Chapter Five

"Jose?" Even with her arms wedged between them, Rafe could feel her shaking as though winter had set in. "Hey."

For a few seconds he did fold his arms around her. She was a perfect fit beneath his chin. Her hair smelled like sweet lemonade and hospital disinfectant. And though the armor he wore beneath his shirt kept him from feeling the curve of her breasts or softness of her cheek resting against his chest, he was completely and instantly aware that the flare of her hip was less pronounced than it had been the last time he'd held her—and her belly was rounder, firmer, fuller, nudging him at his waist.

Holding a woman shouldn't feel this good. The tension in him shouldn't be easing with a sense of rightness and relief at all this body-to-body contact. Not with this woman. Not with…that baby.

Before he lost himself in the mix of new and familiar sensations, before he forgot that he was here for a reason that had nothing to do with touching and wanting, Rafe pulled back. Josie crossed her arms in front of her, still trembling over something that had upset her, and he found he couldn't release her entirely.

He framed her face between his hands, brushing back the loose strands of silky hair that had come free from her ponytail. He hunched down a little to get a good look into her troubled blue eyes. "What's going on? I was waiting until I finished some paperwork after a disturbance we worked this morning to come talk to you, but if you had car trouble, you should have called me sooner."

"I was about to. But this man came over to help me."

"I didn't see any man."

"I know." She was searching again, her distress raising his alertness to the next level. Rafe pulled away and straightened, scanning 360 degrees around the employee entrance and parking lot, looking for anyone showing an interest in Josie. "It's like he vanished. He ducked inside his car or changed his clothes or... He offered to help, but there was just something odd—something off—about him."

"How? What did he say?" Rafe hadn't spotted anyone who seemed out of place. But after that briefing this morning, he wasn't about to dismiss Josie's suspicions.

"He pointed out that I was alone and told me I needed to take better care of my things. Then he called the baby a precious *thing*." She splayed her fingers and slid her palm down over the curve of her belly. "Maybe all these crazy hormones are just making me paranoid."

Rafe pulled his gaze up from the faintly unsettling image of Josie protecting that child. She looked like some kind of proud maternal warrior—fierce, yet vulnerable, beautiful and...his feelings about her being pregnant weren't really part of the equation right now.

Running his fingers over the top of his hair, he took a calming breath.

"One, you're not alone. Two, if you feel there's a threat, act on it. Don't second-guess your instincts or dismiss it as paranoia. And three..." *Take a breath, Delgado.* He needed to set this up just right or Josie would bolt before he had a chance to strike a deal with her. Keeping her safe would be hard enough with Kemp on the loose. Doing it without her cooperation would be damn near impossible. So make nice, *then* lay down the law. "Have you eaten?"

Confusion crinkled beside her eyes. "No. And I need to get to work."

"In a car that doesn't start?" Rafe turned and stooped beneath the hood to check her engine. Stranger? Bad vibe? Serial killer who was a master of disguise? He reached for her hand and tugged her up beside him. "Robbie can wait a few minutes. We need to take care of you right now."

"Oh, don't go all big brother on me." She pulled her hand from his. "I don't have the energy to deal with that right now."

Once he was certain she'd stay close, despite her protests, Rafe turned his attention to the car. It didn't take him five seconds to spot the disconnected cable. He pulled it up and rolled it between his fingers before reattaching it to the battery. The curse he clamped down on hissed between his teeth. "Trust me, *brotherly* isn't what I'm feeling right now."

"What's wrong?"

Rafe clipped the support rod back into place, closed the hood and tucked Josie against his side away from his gun. "Get your bag and get in the truck. We'll drive through someplace for dinner and I'll take you home to change and then to the Shamrock."

"You're not my chauffeur. What about my car? You can't fix it?"

"We'll talk about that, too." Rafe wasn't looking for any man who seemed out of place in the parking lot now—he was looking at every male, trying to match one to the computerized drawing in his head. If the vanishing man was the Rich Girl Killer, then he was every bit as good as Spencer Montgomery had said— and every bit as dangerous and resourceful as his friends Trip Jones and Alex Taylor claimed. Both had worked as bodyguards for two of the women the RGK had stalked. Both women, and his friends, had barely escaped with their lives. "Now move it."

Josie Nichols was neither a lawyer nor an heiress, so there wouldn't be district attorneys or wealthy fathers calling in favors from KCPD and SWAT Team One. But she was getting Rafe's protection. And she was getting it *now*.

"Rafael Delgado, stop!" Josie planted her feet and twisted from his grasp. "Now *you're* the one scaring me."

He opened her car door, grabbed her bag, grabbed her elbow and didn't wait for any argument as he turned her toward the truck. "You need to be scared. Your car was sabotaged. Battery cables can corrode over time and break, but they don't disconnect and grow tool marks all by themselves."

Her cheeks blanched, but she was nodding, moving. "That's all you needed to say. Was that so hard?"

"Didn't you once tell me that words weren't my best thing?" he challenged as he helped her into the passenger seat, dropped her bag beside her feet and reached across her for the seat belt.

"Yes, but I also believe you're a smart enough man to learn a few considerations beyond giving orders and manhandling people."

It was impossible to miss how her hands came up to catch the seat belt and keep it—and him—from touching her stomach. Fine. Point taken. He supposed she'd added him to the list of things she had to protect her baby from. Ignoring the withering feeling that felt a little like the first time he'd realized his home life wasn't like most of the other kids' he went to school with, and that he'd never truly fit in, he gentled his movements and apologized. "Sorry. *Manhandling* you was never my intention. Getting you out of harm's way *is*."

"I know that, Rafe." She covered his hand with hers, offering a healing understanding that his parents had never shown him. "One thing I've never doubted about you is that you always have my best interests at heart. I just wish you would let your... Never mind." She patted his hand and pulled away. "I'll admit I was a little scared. But you think I had reason to be, right?"

Oh, yeah. If she only knew.

Acknowledging the temporary truce with a nod, he closed the door and climbed in behind the wheel to start the 3500's powerful engine. "I replaced your battery myself last winter. I clean the nodes every time I change your oil. Someone definitely got under the hood and took things apart so the engine wouldn't start. I'll call the lab and Detective Montgomery to take a look at it."

As soon as he turned onto the street and pulled up to the stoplight, she moaned. "I'm feeling a little sick to my stomach."

Rafe pressed more lightly on the accelerator when the light changed. "Calling Montgomery is just a precaution. You're safe for now."

"It's not just stress. Or your driving. Oh." Her teasing smile became a grimace as they crested a hill and went down the other side. "It's the baby."

His grip tightened around the steering wheel as a bolt of panic shot through him. "Is something wrong? Do I need to get you back to the hospital?"

Josie laughed, a sound he hadn't heard in his company for far too many months now. "No. I'm hungry. Junior likes to eat about six times a day or he tells me about it."

"It's a he?" The panic eased at her laugh, but his knuckles were still white. He was having a son?

"The *baby*," she clarified, "could be a boy or girl. I asked the doctor's office not to tell me when they did the ultrasound."

A picture of a dark-haired little girl toddling into his arms distracted him for only a moment before he quashed the image beneath practicality and set aside that gut-kick of emotion. "When was the last time you ate anything?"

"I had a sandwich at noon."

Over five hours ago, his dashboard clock winked at him. That was too long between meals even if she wasn't eating for two. Rafe quickly scanned the road ahead and pulled off onto the shoulder as soon as it was safe. Then he shifted the idling pickup into Park and reached behind the seat for the truck's emergency kit.

"What are you doing?" she asked.

Beneath a roll of sterile gauze, he pulled out a protein bar and tossed it into her lap. "Eat."

"Rafe, I was uncomfortable. It's an empty tummy, not a life or death situation."

"Eat it, anyway, until we can get a cheeseburger and a milkshake in you."

"Thank you." He waited for her to unwrap the bar and take a bite, blow out a sigh that rounded her lips, and lean back against the headrest in weary relief before he put away the plastic tub and shifted the truck into gear. "Actually, I've been craving vegetables," she announced as another bite disappeared.

"Not pickles and ice cream?"

"Nothing weird, yet. Although I won't be eating a tuna casserole for a while. The last time I opened a packet of tuna, the smell made me sick to my stomach."

Rafe checked the side view mirror and concentrated on merging back into rush-hour traffic. Did he need to know the details about her pregnancy? Should these little nuggets of info about the gender of the baby, its snack habits and Josie's needs and cravings really be sneaking their way beneath his skin and feeding something inside him that he hadn't known was just as hungry as she was? Had to be curiosity, that was all. He'd never had any firsthand experience with pregnant women, and his only experience with fatherhood had been a history he'd spent years in therapy trying to forget.

There was no way he could become attached to the baby—Aaron's grandson, no less—without screwing up this relationship the way he had with anybody else he'd cared about in his life.

It was vitally important that he regain Josie's trust. If he was going to provide the protection Spencer Montgomery would not, then he needed her to listen to him. To act when he told her to, and not second-guess any of the rules he intended to lay down for her safety until the killer she could identify was caught. And he needed to focus strictly on the danger at hand.

He wouldn't let babies and emotions and this rift between them get in the way of that.

So he'd stick to the black and white practicalities that he could deal with best. "There's a take-out salad bar in that grocery store up on Noland Road," he pointed out, pulling the truck into the turn lane. "Do you want me to stop there?"

"That'd be great," she answered between chews. "Although that milkshake does sound good. Can I have both?"

A smile curved the corner of his mouth. That was the Josie he remembered, full of healthy appetites and honest to a fault. By the time they'd cruised the salad bar and driven through a fast-food restaurant for shakes and a burger for him, Josie seemed happy and amenable to the conversation they needed to have.

Her vanilla milkshake was half gone by the time Rafe had maneuvered his truck into a parking space in front of Josie's apartment building. He shut off the engine and pocketed the key. The sun was dropping in his rearview mirror and she'd be wanting to get to the

Shamrock as soon as she could wolf down that salad and change. The time to do this was now. "Do you think it was him?"

Josie was too smart to ask what *him* he was talking about. "You think the man in the hospital parking lot was the Rich Girl Killer?" She pulled the straw and ice cream from her lips, dabbing with a paper napkin while her youthful exuberance aged and grew thoughtful. "I don't know. I never suspected it was the same guy. I didn't get a good look at his face. But, now that I think about it, he didn't want me to. They both wore glasses, but different styles. The hair was different. The guy at the prison had money, like an attorney, you know, all spit and polish. This guy was casual—with a ball cap and tennis shoes…"

Her gaze grew distant, remembering something horrible, imagining something worse. "Jose?" Rafe reached across the seat and touched her arm, the contact snapping her out of her disquieting thoughts.

"They both had the cleanest hands I've ever seen on a man." Ah, hell. That fit Montgomery's profile. Judging by the color draining from Josie's cheeks, she was beginning to think that, too. She unbuckled and turned to face him across the cab. "If that was him, why didn't he just shoot me or stab me right there?"

He slipped his hand down the sleeve of her cotton jacket and squeezed her fingers. "I, for one, am glad he didn't."

"You know what I mean. If he could get to me like that, why didn't he do something?"

"Either he saw me coming and thought he'd have a witness, or…"

"Or what?" She turned her smaller palm into his, lacing their fingers together, waiting expectantly for the grim news.

"He's toying with you. That's been his M.O. with his victims—stalk, torment, then attack." Rafe rubbed his calloused thumb over the cool skin of her knuckles, wanting to make her aware, not afraid. "This guy's sick. He isn't playing with a full deck."

Her fingers danced nervously between his. "But Detective Montgomery promised to keep my name out of it. It's not even written in his case file—he showed me. How could the RGK know I was the witness? How did he know where to find me?"

"If he can con his way into a prison to kill a man, he could get into a university or hospital and search its records." Rafe offered another distasteful explanation. "He saw you with Patrick. Maybe he has connections inside there who got the info for him."

"From Patrick? Would he hurt him, too?"

In a heartbeat. Half of the RGK's victims were expendable associates or innocents who'd gotten between him and his target.

Rafe didn't have to answer out loud. Josie knew. She pulled her hand from his and hugged her arm around her baby before opening the door and heading up the sidewalk to her building. Rafe was out of the truck and by her side in an instant, glimpsing into every car and shaded window surrounding them as they walked into the lobby and buzzed for the elevator. Despite the stiffness with which she carried herself, he kept his hand at the small of her back, a visual reminder to any curious eyes that this woman was not alone in the world—that anyone who intended to do her harm would have to get through him first.

Once the elevator doors closed, he let her move away and sag against the railing on the opposite side of the elevator car.

But the mix of hope and despair in her eyes tore right through him, even from a distance. "The man at my car might not have been the Rich Girl Killer. He could have been just a random creepy guy."

"Hanging around you? I don't like that much better."

She pulled her shoulders back and walked to the doors as the elevator's ascent slowed. Even with her back squarely facing him, he recognized her bravado for what it was. "Well, fortunately, it's not your problem. I know what you're up to, Rafe. And I can't have you shadowing me 24/7, bossing me around and playing bodyguard."

"It's either that or a safe house."

Her ponytail serpentined down her back as she shook her head. "I'm in my last few weeks of school. I have to work to pay bills and get everything ready for the baby. I can't be locked away."

She'd bite his head off for this one, but he had to make the offer. "I'll cover any income you might miss, pay for anything you or the baby needs while you're in the safe house."

"Oh, no, you don't, Sergeant Delgado." She wagged her finger at him. "I know you think you're doing me a favor, but money is the last thing I want from you. You are not going to turn what's left of our friendship into the Josie Nichols charity."

What's left...? He really had messed up with her,

hadn't he, if she mistook his concern for charity. "Then I guess you've got yourself a bodyguard."

The doors opened and she headed down the thinly carpeted hallway, with Rafe striding right behind her. "That's ridiculous. You have to work. We have different schedules. Now that I know this guy may have found me, I promise I won't take any chances. I grew up around cops and a criminal both, Rafe—I know how to be careful. I'll add another lock to the door, make sure someone I know is always with me when I'm away from home, let people know my destination and when I should be there." She glanced over her shoulder before pulling out her keys. "How about we compromise and I still let you walk me to my car every night?"

"That's a given."

He let her have one harrumph of frustration before urging her to unlock the door. Once they were inside, he closed and bolted it while she dropped her bag on a chair and marched into the kitchen to grab a fork and eat a few bites of her salad. She went into the bathroom and Rafe checked the window in her living room that led onto the fire escape. He made sure the closet in her bedroom was clear, and the window there was secure, too.

He was kneeling over a stack of oak slats, railings and steel hardware in the corner of her bedroom when she came in behind him. "See? We're managing just fine without you," she claimed, tossing her jacket onto the bed and pulling a pair of jeans and a striped blouse from her closet.

Rafe was looking at a hodgepodge of crib parts with a few nicks in the wood, a plastic bag full of nuts and bolts and no visible set of instructions. At least the plastic-wrapped mattress looked new and intact. "How did you get this all up here?"

"I carried it. Since the shop didn't have a box for the crib, it took me a few trips, but I made it."

"You should have called me."

"To help with the baby?" She plucked the bag of parts from his hand and set it beside the heap of wood pieces. "Like I said, I absolve you of all responsibility. I'm not looking for a handyman, either."

Rafe pushed to his feet, catching her arm and turning her to face him, stopping her in the middle of kicking off her shoes. "No arguments on this, Jose. Your anonymity's a thing of the past. Montgomery may think keeping a low profile and all your dad's friends at the Shamrock are enough to keep you safe from that bastard, but I've seen what the guy can do. He's a damn chameleon. Like today at the hospital. You don't even know he's there until it's too late." He threaded his fingers into the sable-colored silk of her ponytail where it fell over her shoulder, and let just a little of his own frustration and fear bubble to the surface. "I can't handle *too late* with you."

"Because of the promise you made to Dad?" Reaching up, she cupped her hand against the pulse beating alongside his jaw, the gentleness of the gesture warming his skin, soothing his pain, making him wish he could give her what she needed. "You made that promise to my father when I was fifteen years old, Rafe. I'm a grown woman now. Isn't there any promise you want to make to me?"

The back of his knuckles brushed over the swell of

a small breast that was firmer, fuller than he remembered. "I promise to keep you safe."

Her lips parted and her breath caught on a barely audible gasp when he couldn't help but repeat the caress. Her blue eyes tilted toward his. "And the baby?"

"Yeah. That, too."

"That? It? We created a human being, Rafe, not a thing. I can't imagine what you must have endured growing up that makes you so afraid of caring." Her eyes sparkled with a hint of moisture, but her posture rebuffed the impulse to pull her into his arms to deny the accusation and console her big heart. Rafe buried the urge to hold her altogether when she tugged her hair from his fingers and tossed her ponytail behind her back. She gave him a slight shove to push him out into the living room and close the door between them. "Give me a couple of minutes to change and then you can drive me to the Shamrock."

Rafe stood there as the door closed in his face. He wanted nothing more than to push it back open and either hash it out with Josie or haul her into his arms and kiss her until this raging frustration left his system and he could get back to being the man who'd once joked so easily with her, the man who was welcome to take her hand or touch her hair or lend some help or just spend a quiet evening in the peace and acceptance and joie de vivre that was Josie Nichols.

He shot his fingers through his hair with a curse and paced across the tiny apartment. Yeah, like that was going to happen. He'd betrayed his word to Aaron and messed up what he had with Josie the night he'd slept with her.

But he'd been so raw with Calvin Chambers's death, so riddled with guilt. So damn helpless when he'd devoted his life to fixing what was wrong in the world and saving people. That could have been him a lifetime ago—a wounded child, helpless and friendless—in so much pain, yet filled with a futile hope. Rafe had hurt so bad that night and he'd turned to Josie. The person who knew him best. His friend. His solace.

Now he'd given her the burden of a baby. Another child he was afraid to get attached to, afraid he'd fail. Then there was this damn murder, and Josie had had the dumb luck to be the one person who could identify the man KCPD had been tracking for two years. She shouldn't have to deal with any of this.

He had so much to atone for. So much to make right. So much he needed, but couldn't have and shouldn't want—and it was all back there, behind that closed bedroom door.

Rafe stopped in his tracks, braced his hands on his hips and tilted his head back, venting his frustration to the ceiling. "Tell me what I'm supposed to do, Aaron."

The walls in Josie's apartment were so thin that even though he tried to politely tune out the sounds, he heard what could have been a sniffle or a curse coming from her bedroom. There was a shuffle of movement, the squeak of the mattress as she sat on the bed, a telltale beep as she pushed her answering machine to play her messages.

He had plenty to think about to keep him from eavesdropping on a message about her work schedule at the medical center and an appointment reminder from her OB/GYN. But good intentions and errant hormones and unfamiliar feelings couldn't distract him from the third message. The cop in him responded to the male voice, the false apology, the inherent threat.

"I'm sorry things didn't work out for us at the hospital, Josie. Pity, really—you seem like such a nice young woman. I've never gotten that close to someone who was pregnant before. What's that like, feeling something growing inside you? I wish I had more time to get better acquainted with you and the baby. But I'm afraid business must come first. Don't worry, though. I promise we'll be meeting again...when there's no one around to interrupt us."

Rafe was inside Josie's bedroom before the message ended. He found her half-dressed, hugging the blouse against her chest. Her eyes were huge, her voice a whisper when she turned to him. "Rafe?"

"Pack your bag."

Chapter Six

Josie startled at the tweak on her ponytail, but quickly exhaled a calming breath and smiled at the deep brogue that trilled against her ear.

"Hey, girlie." Uncle Robbie hugged her shoulders and reached across her to steal a pretzel from the bowl on the bar and pop it into his mouth. "You're mighty jumpy this evening. Everything all right?"

"I'm fine." Josie dumped the dregs of two beers into the sink behind the bar and set the pilsners into the crate with the glasses she'd been rinsing. "I just have lots on my mind tonight."

Like that phone call at her apartment. If she hadn't already been creeped out by the mystery man at the hospital, the message might have been a casual flirtation. But someone had sabotaged her car. The surgeon in the ball cap had appeared and vanished like magic. And then that unsettling call—on her line, at *her* home—had mentioned the baby. Somehow, his curiosity about her pregnancy intensified the threat and gave the subtext behind that message a more disturbing meaning.

Josie felt a dampness against her belly and snapped from her thoughts when she realized her wet, sudsy hand had soaked through her blouse, maternity jeans and panties where she had instinctively protected her child. "Oh, shoot." She flicked the suds off her hands and reached for a towel.

"Is everything all right with Junior?" he asked, stepping back to give her room to dab at her clothes.

"The baby's fine, too."

"Still no help from that no-good father whose name you won't tell me?"

More help than she wished, actually.

"Give it a rest, Robbie."

The last thing she wanted was for Rafe's friendship with her uncle to splinter the way theirs had. She'd grown up in a fractured family and knew how important it was to maintain ties with every person she cared about. And Rafe had no one, really, besides his friends on SWAT Team One. And her. But he'd made it more than plain that he didn't want her—or rather, that he didn't want to want her. He certainly didn't want the baby. And since they were a package deal, she was beginning to lose hope that her longtime fantasy of sharing a life with Rafe Delgado would ever come true.

Robbie shifted back and forth on his feet beside her, then cleared his throat. Josie turned her head to see what topic this natural-born blarney man was having such a difficult time with.

"What?" she asked.

He cleared his throat again. "Well, I was just thinking. If this nonexistent man of yours could help you with some money... I won't be able to give you the bonus I was hoping to, this month."

"It's all right, Robbie," she assured him, "I'm not expecting you to support us."

If anything, her reassurance seemed to sadden him. "But I want to help with the wee one." A moment later, his broad smile returned. "I did hear about a job you'd be right for. Got a call looking for help just this evening. A catering company is hiring wait staff to set up and clear tables for that big fundraiser KCPD is throwing later this month."

Another job on her feet. Great. But at least it was a job, and for that, Josie was grateful. And since there'd be any number of cops in attendance, Rafe should agree to let her work without too much argument. Josie smiled her thanks as one of the waitresses brought her another tray of empties. "Just give me the time and the place. And thanks."

"Things are about to get busy," her uncle warned her, pointing to the nine o'clock newscast starting on the television hanging above the end of the bar. "Do you need to take a break before KCPD's A shift ends and our friends come in here to unwind?"

The end of A shift. That meant Rafe would be coming back soon.

Yeah, she definitely needed some quiet time to regroup for the next encounter with the man who'd turned her life upside down in so many ways. She balanced the two glasses on top of the full crate and heaved it up into her arms. "I'll go start a load in through the dishwasher."

"Wait. Let Jake take it." Robbie lifted the crate from Josie's hands and called to the man moving bar stools back into place around the two pool tables near the opposite side of the bar. "Jake?"

She felt a chill dance along her spine as Robbie's

shout momentarily silenced the hum of conversations at the tables. But the patrons quickly went back to their business, the noise level increased and a muscular man with a buzz cut of hair wound his way across the room to join them.

"Have you met Jake Lonergan?" Robbie asked as the new help approached. "I took your advice and hired someone new."

Jake Lonergan didn't look like any bartender she knew. As he stooped beneath the opening at the end of the bar and approached, the details of his face became a little more clear, though not any friendlier. His un-smiling features belonged to a bouncer who'd not only broken up, but had been in one too many fights himself. A vague uneasiness backed her into Robbie's chest, but curiosity made her peer into the dim light and blinding neon of the advertisement signs around them to see if that bump on his crooked nose or that scar along his jaw were makeup or the real thing.

"Jake, this is my niece, Josie. Here." Robbie handed the heavy crate of dirty glasses off to the stocky man. "I want you to run them through the washer in the back. Bring out a clean set and fill up the cooler to chill the glasses when you come back."

"Ma'am." Jake shrugged off the impolite scrutiny, took the crate and carried the dirty glasses through the swinging door back into the kitchen.

Josie hadn't been able to get a good look at his eyes with the perpetual squint lining them. And that not knowing bothered her almost more than seeing the cold, colorless eyes of a killer would have.

"Now go," Robbie ordered, squeezing her shoulders

and pressing a kiss to her cheek. "You're shaking on your feet. Sit down in my office and relax for ten minutes."

Alone in the back of the bar with a man she'd just met? No, thanks.

When Jake came back out, she'd apologize for her rudeness and strike up a conversation so she could get a better look at him. Her nerves wouldn't settle until she was satisfied the new bartender wasn't the RGK with a new disguise and the guts or arrogance to track her down in a bar surrounded by cops. She couldn't imagine Donny Kemp would risk working in a bar where two-thirds of the patrons were employees of the Kansas City police department. But then, twenty-four hours ago, she wouldn't have believed he could find out where she was doing her nursing practicum and call her home phone number, either.

A slap on the bar's polished walnut top took her uncle's attention away and Josie went back to work. "Robbie, you old dog, how's it going?"

"Norbert." Robbie traded a robust handshake with the retired cop who'd been a customer at the Shamrock since before Josie's time. With a tilt of his head, Robbie urged his friend to an empty stool at the end of the bar and filled him a draft along the way. "You got any good tips for me tonight, Norb? I've got a couple grand I need to make up."

"They've started the horse races in Virginia and Ohio this month. Manny's taking bets over at the keno hall if you want me to…"

Gambling. Josie shook her head in frustration and tuned out the conversation. So it wasn't the new help but an old habit that had eaten up Robbie's bonus money this month.

Needing to busy her hands more than she needed to rest or worry about her uncle, Josie pulled an apron off a hook beside the swinging door and slipped it over her head, tying the strings behind her back and adding another layer of protection between her baby and the perils of her world. After wiping down the hoses and dispensers for their soft drinks, the bell over the door alerted her to the pair of detectives wandering in and heading over to their usual corner near the pool tables.

Spencer Montgomery and his partner, Nick Fensom. The two of them were like night and day—Montgomery with his light red, almost strawberry-blond hair versus Detective Fensom's dark brown hair. Montgomery was suited up while Fensom wore jeans and a bomber jacket. One was tall and lean, the other a shorter, muscle-packed bulldog of a man.

Neither detective looked like the man at her car this afternoon. But then that sham surgeon, if he was, indeed, the RGK, hadn't looked anything like the man she'd seen at the prison, either. Should she tell them her suspicions about Jake Lonergan? Let them know that the RGK—if that was the man who'd called her and sabotaged her car—had gotten so deep inside her head that she was even sizing up the cops she'd known for years as regular customers and friends of her father's as possible suspects?

She knew she'd been staring too long when the red-haired detective made eye contact and his gaze narrowed with a silent question. Then he held up two fingers, indicating their order for a pair of draft beers.

She let her gaze wander from table to table and shadow to shadow across the bar. Was the RGK here now? Blending in? Watching her? Maybe it wasn't wise to indicate that she knew Spencer Montgomery outside of the police station. Any interested observer might wonder why the detective was suddenly talking to her and piece together that she was involved in his investigation, that *she* could be his anonymous witness. Or would it draw less attention to fix a tray of drinks and carry them over like she would with any other customer?

Falling back on the diversion of work, she drew the two drafts and set them on a tray. Was she going to be jumpy and suspicious of every man she met now?

She'd thought the cold, conscienceless gaze she'd seen behind those glasses at the prison visitation room belonged to eyes she'd never forget. But if the RGK had sabotaged her car and spoken to her this afternoon—she hadn't recognized him. Would she ever be able to? Would she be able to identify the killer she'd seen before it was too late? The niggling doubts made her worry that all of Rafe's dire predictions about the danger she was in might come true.

She wasn't particularly looking forward to spending the night at Rafe's apartment. He'd tossed her suitcase into the back of his truck, driven her to the Shamrock and then returned to KCPD for the last couple of hours of his shift with stern instructions that she was not to leave the bar, be alone with anyone she didn't know, or take any phone calls until he could get there.

While she was grateful for the protective streak that ran a mile deep inside Rafe, she couldn't help but wish there was a more personal reason for his round-the-clock attention. Someday she'd have to get over these feelings for Rafael Delgado. She'd have to move past the futile hope that he would one day see her as a woman instead of Aaron Nichols's daughter—that Rafe would see her as *his* woman.

Sucker. Every ding of the bell over the Shamrock's doorway felt like a death knell counting down what was left of her foolish, hopeful heart. Of all the men in the world to see as her soul mate, she had to fall for one who was hard to love—a man whose wounds ran so deep that there might never be enough patience and time to heal them.

"Order up for table twelve," Josie announced, carrying the tray to the waitress station at the end of the bar.

"Table twelve can wait." The gravelly masculine voice jump-started Josie's pulse and put the brakes on the downward spiral of her thoughts.

"Rafe." So much for logical future plans and declarations of independence. The heart wanted what it wanted. And right now, it wanted to believe that the liquid warmth she saw burning in Rafe's whiskey-colored eyes was triggered by caring. Her heart shouldn't lurch in her chest at the sight of the tall, uniformed man in black standing just a few feet away from her, his eyes skimming every nuance of her face and figure from head to toe.

"You doin' okay?" he asked in a voice that floated beneath the expanding noise level of the crowd for her ears alone.

She nodded.

But he didn't look entirely convinced. His gaze darted beyond her to the detectives by the pool tables and back. Rafe's fingers brushed against hers as he took the tray from her grasp. "Did Montgomery say something to upset you?"

"He just ordered a couple of beers."

"These?"

Josie nodded.

"You take care of your customers here. I'll deliver them to your friend." He picked up the tray and dodged out of the waitress's way. "I need to have a few words with him, anyway. He needs to know about that phone call."

"Rafe?" Did she really want him antagonizing Detective Montgomery? Would watchful eyes have seen Rafe talking to her and then connect her to Montgomery's investigation? She surveyed the crowd filling booths and tables, setting up pool shots and waiting to place orders. But there were too many faces, too many distractions. Squeezing her eyes shut, Josie shook her head, struggling to recapture her serenity and trust in the world she'd lost earlier today.

"Excuse me. It's Josie, right?" A woman's voice intruded on her brief meditation. Josie blinked her eyes open and crossed to the blonde in a black SWAT uniform that matched Rafe's. "I'm Randy—Miranda—Murdock. Are you feeling okay?"

Did she really look such a mess that everyone in the bar was going to ask her that tonight?

Deciding she was tired of answering the question, Josie pasted what she hoped was a convincing smile on her face and ignored giving an answer. "I remember you, Randy." She looked off into the corner of the bar where the rest of SWAT Team One—Captain Michael Cutler, Trip Jones and Alex Taylor—were pulling chairs up to their regular table. With familiar friends in the house, it was easier to turn her smile into the real thing. "I'm guessing you're here to order a round of the usual for the guys?"

"It's like having a pack of big brothers," Randy groused, laying a twenty dollar bill on top of the bar. "Like I need four more of them. I already have one who's got the overprotective angle down to a science. You get that big brother act from Sergeant Delgado, don't you? Can't they see we're grown women?"

Josie's gaze darted to Rafe, whose dark head was bent forward to press some point, on her behalf, no doubt, with Detective Montgomery. "I think it's just born in some men to be protectors."

Randy was on a roll, carrying the conversation for both of them. "I carry a rifle for my job. You handle all this chaos with a smile on your face. And they still think we need looking after?"

"Are you having any luck changing their minds?"

Randy shook her head. "Some days yes, some days no. I just keep at it. I keep doing my job, being tough. Hopefully, one day, it'll get through their thick skulls that we can take care of ourselves." The other woman paused for a breath and grinned. "I'm rambling. Sorry. I tend to go off at the mouth when I get fired up about something."

"No problem. Half my job is listening." Josie reached into the cooler to pull out five frosty pilsner glasses to fill the order. "Did something happen today to set the big brothers off?"

Tucking a strand of honey-blond hair behind her ear, Randy nodded. "We just came back from a walk-through at a Gallagher Security warehouse. An anonymous tipster called in a bomb threat."

Bombs in Kansas City? And Rafe was in the middle of it? Josie's glasses clinked together as her fingers shook. "Was anyone hurt?"

"Nope. Gallagher's security chief evacuated the building and we cleared it. Or I should say the boys did. My job was to stay by the door and watch the crowd—safely out of harm's way."

"They were trusting you to take care of those innocent bystanders so they could focus on the job they were doing inside."

"I guess. I mean, I know it's all about teamwork. But I train just as hard as they do. I shoot better than all of them. And *I* get stuck on door duty? Makes me wonder if they'll ever trust me to pull the trigger when the time comes."

"And the bomb?" Josie steadied her hand and filled the next glass.

"Even when we brought a dog in, we never found anything. I guess it really disrupted the end of the workday, though, and some shipment they were trying to get out."

"From what I read in the papers, Quinn Gallagher can afford to lose a day's work and delay shipments. I'm just glad everyone's safe." Josie set the last frothy glass on a tray and put it in front of Officer Murdock. "Here you go."

"Thanks for letting me vent." Randy held out the twenty.

Josie refused the money. "We've got a few traditions here at the Shamrock. One, you listen when someone needs to vent. And two, the first round's on the house any day you survive a dangerous situation like you faced today. I think eliminating a bomb threat definitely qualifies."

"I appreciate you listening, Josie. I don't have that many girlfriends to talk to—and none of them who understand police work. And somehow, I just don't think a guy gets what we're feeling." Randy got up from her stool and, after a moment's hesitation, dropped the twenty dollars into the tip jar. "Good luck with Sarge and that whole big brother thing."

"You, too."

Before the empty stool filled with the next customer, Josie stole another look at Rafe, deep in conversation with Montgomery and Fensom. She understood from her father, and the men and women who frequented the bar, that even when they faced a deadly situation like a bomb threat, they were just doing their job. But she also understood that when things were particularly tense, that those same cops needed to commiserate, celebrate—or vent about the day's events like Miranda Murdock just had.

Like the night Rafe had needed her body and her caring to help him deal with the senseless murder of a little boy who'd died in his arms.

Tonight, instead of decompressing the stress of the job with his buddies, and toasting their success after a potentially deadly mission, Rafe's first concern had been about her.

It was enough to keep the hope in her heart from dying.

Chapter Seven

The grapefruit sitting on her bladder demanded that Josie quit trying to make the numbers add up on the deposit slip she'd been filling out and go to the bathroom *now*.

"Come on, Junior, work with me," she begged, hopping to her feet and pressing her thighs together to give herself a few extra seconds to zip the money sheet into the bag with the cash from the registers tonight. Normally, her uncle was here to take the deposit to the bank, but he'd disappeared after last call and she hadn't seen him since. With her bladder winning the war against her determination to finish counting down the drawers, she tossed the bag into Robbie's safe and spun the dial before darting out of the office.

"Look out," a gruff voice called as she swung the door open.

"Excuse me." She scooted past Jake Lonergan and the flats of beer he was carrying out of the walk-in fridge.

There was still no hint of recognition, which should have been a good thing. But until she could sit him down in the daylight and look into his eyes, she wasn't going to spend any more time getting acquainted than she had to. Besides, Junior was demanding her attention right now.

A few minutes and a clearer head later, Josie stood at the bathroom door, wondering if Robbie had come back, any of the waitresses had stayed late or Jake had gone home. Perhaps staying after closing to fill out paperwork wasn't the wisest thing to do anymore, especially if her only company was a man she didn't know.

If Jake Lonergan was the RGK in disguise, and they *were* alone, he could have sliced and diced her and been long gone by now. So, it was probably safe to go out this door. But Rafe had said that the elusive serial killer liked to stalk his victims first—torment them right up to the moment he killed them.

Standing here in the tiny bathroom with her hand on the knob, unsure whether or not to unlock this door—wishing she'd brought her cell phone or a security camera or some psychic intuition with her—was definitely torture.

A sharp rap on the door startled her back a step. "Josie?" Rafe's deep voice called with another knock. "Josie, you in there?"

Relief rushed in as the initial stab of adrenaline ebbed away. With a steadying breath and a teasing smile, she opened the door to a wall of Rafe Delgado's chest. Her gasp of surprise filled her nose with his woodsy, masculine scent and made her voice breathy. "Yes?"

Her body warmed with an instant, primal heat. His arms were braced against the door frame on either side of her, the black sleeves of his uniform rolled up to expose his sinewy forearms. A late-night stubble shadowed the sexy angles of his jaw and mouth. If only that mouth was smiling. "Are you all right? You were in there for almost ten minutes."

A gentle push to the center of his chest urged him back and gave her brain a chance to assert itself over the rapid-fire beat of her pulse. She turned down the hallway. "What, you're timing my potty breaks now?"

Rafe followed her into Robbie's office. "You done here tonight? It's after one. We've both had a long day."

"Just a few details left." She untied her apron and pulled it off over her head. "How did your conversation with Detective Montgomery go?"

He moved aside a stack of papers and sat on the front edge of Robbie's walnut desk while Josie circled behind it to drape her apron over the chair and reopen the safe. "Montgomery said the lab found a half dozen prints on your car. Mine, for sure. Yours. And the others he's running through the system to see if we can get a hit. Although they've never recovered any usable prints from the RGK's crime scenes, so I don't know what he's comparing them to. I've got him running a background check on Lonergan, too. I don't like the timing of a new guy entering your life when all this is going on."

"Are you going to be investigating every man I meet?"

"If he gives you a weird vibe or makes you think of Donny Kemp in any way, yes. I want to find this guy before he finds you."

So her suspicions of the new bartender had been that obvious? If it turned out to be nothing, she'd owe Jake a serious apology for being so uncharacteristically unwelcoming. Josie took her time to double-check that the low numbers she'd come up with were correct, then tucked the deposit slip and cash back into the safe. She'd worked for her uncle long enough to know what the intake for an average night should look like, and the cash just wasn't there.

"Have you seen Robbie?" she asked, wondering if Rafe could read the concern she was feeling on that topic as well.

"Not since he locked the front door." He raised his gaze, indicating the apartment above them. "Did he turn in already?"

"Without taking the deposit to the bank or saying good-night?"

Rafe pulled out his phone. "Do you want me to call him?"

"Please." While he punched in the number, Josie saved the order forms on Robbie's computer and powered down the system. Then she pulled a sheet of paper from the printer to write him a note.

"Voice mail. We'll run up and check on him when you're done here." Rafe snapped his phone shut and returned it to the clip on his belt. "I also told Montgomery you'd be staying with me indefinitely."

She looked up at the stark pronouncement. "What did he say to that?"

"I wasn't asking his permission."

Josie signed her love to her uncle and pushed away from the desk. "Why do I get the idea that the two of you don't get along?"

"I didn't hide the fact that I disapprove of how he's handling you as a witness. He should have put you in a safe house from the moment you gave him that description of the RGK." A hint of teasing colored his husky voice, making him sound, for the moment, like the old Rafe. "But then you probably wouldn't have cooperated with him any more than you have with me, right?"

That earned him a little smile when she circled around the desk to face him. "I'm stubbornly independent. What can I say?"

"It's that Irish blood. You need a little more Italian running through you to melt some of that bullheadedness."

Her smile softened into something serene and she touched her belly knowingly. She *had* some Italian genes growing inside her now.

"Does it hurt?" Rafe's voice was little more than a gravelly whisper.

"What? Being pregnant?"

"I picked up a book after dinner tonight, but I haven't had a chance to read it." Rafe Delgado bought a book on pregnancy? Did she dare think his interest was personal and not practical? "Is that why you were in the john so long? Are you suffering any because of what I've done to you?"

The tortured doubts shading his eyes crumbled the fragile armor she'd been building around her heart. Could he really think this baby was some sort of penance she had to bear for the needy, unguarded night they'd shared six months ago? He hadn't been alone in that truck. True, this pregnancy wasn't planned, but she couldn't imagine herself carrying anyone else's baby. It might be the only part of Rafe he'd ever let her love the way she wanted to.

"You need to read that book," she advised, crossing to where he sat on the edge of the desk. His knees parted and she walked between them to cradle the line of his jaw in the warmth of her palms. "Everything is completely normal. The baby and I are healthy, and the pregnancy is progressing just the way it should." She stroked her thumb across the stubbled point of his chin, trying to ease the tension she felt in him. "Sure, I had some morning sickness, which isn't too pleasant. But that's done. I'm getting stretch marks and I had to switch to maternity clothes because my regular things were getting too tight. I get a twinge in the small of my back when I've been on my feet too long—something about my balance being off. My fingers and ankles swell sometimes, but not anything like they're expected to in that last month. So far, it's all boringly normal. Thank goodness."

He threaded his long fingers into her ponytail, studying the long, wavy strands for a moment before tilting his gaze straight into hers. "Jose, I'm so sorry. I never meant for my out-of-control needs to make things so miserable for you."

"I'm not miserable at all."

"But you just said—"

"Shh." She covered his mouth with her fingers, noting the contrast between his supple lips and the coarser skin surrounding them, just as she noted the mix of pain and apology in his eyes. "Being pregnant is a wonderful adventure. Every day brings something new. I can feel the baby move now, did you know that? I have pictures from the ultrasound, but I can't tell if it's a boy or a girl yet." Her laugh sounded low and sensual to her own ears as she shared these intimate details with him for the first time. "Heck, without my obstetrics class, I'd have hardly been able to tell it was a baby. But the nurse-midwife has her suspicions."

His hands settled on her hips as he leaned back to look down at her belly. The hardness beside his eyes softened with a bit of boyish wonder. "You can feel the baby?"

"Sometimes. Especially when I'm trying to rest. That's when the little one seems to want to have a party. Here." She pulled his hand from her hip and lifted her blouse to guide him to the elastic panel of her jeans.

But a hail storm of glass breaking near the back door, followed by a wail of angry shouts, ended the lesson before Rafe could touch her.

Rafe shot to his feet, pulling her behind him and warning her with his hand to stay put while he unstrapped the holster on his thigh and dashed down the hallway with his hand resting on the butt of his gun. The startling violence of sound left her frozen in place, nodding her understanding.

Until Rafe swung open the back door and disappeared outside.

Until she heard her uncle shout a curse that ended with the ear-chafing grind of the trash bin slamming into the bricks and a moan of pain.

"Robbie?" He was hurt. Her feet were moving.

"I paid what I had—"

"Do you understand?" a strange voice warned.

"KCPD! Get down on the ground!" Rafe shouted.

Josie ran to the shattered door in time to see Rafe fly

at one of the two men beating her uncle to the ground in the parking lot behind the bar.

The two men hit the pavement hard and rolled.

"Sammy! Move it! Move it!" The second man dashed to a waiting car, its doors wide open, its engine running and ready for a quick getaway.

A meaty fist clipped Rafe's chin, knocking him off the first man. The bald muscular man pushed to his knees. "Damn it, Marco, wait for me!"

The black-haired man named Marco stopped in his tracks and wheeled around. She saw a flash of shiny metal slide from Marco's jacket. She heard Robbie moan. Rafe kicked out with his legs and snaked his feet around the bald man's knees, toppling him to the ground. Marco charged.

Josie's stomach plummeted to her toes. "Oh, my God…stop! Stop it!"

"Josie!" Rafe cursed, grunted, picked the smaller man up and slammed him to the ground.

"Get out of here, girlie!" Robbie clawed his fingers into the bricks and tried to stand. His eye was swollen, his mouth bleeding. "It's none…your concern."

When he collapsed, Josie ran to him, wedging her shoulder beneath his arm and pushing with her legs. "Get up!"

Marco changed course. "Yeah, girlie. Get out of here."

Josie pushed harder. "Come on!"

Robbie found a hand grip on the wall and got his legs beneath him. Rafe jammed his knee in the middle of the bald man's back. "Josie!" he rasped. "Get inside!"

The glint of metal took the shape of a knife in Josie's

peripheral vision. They were nearly at the door when she felt the hand in her hair. "Unless you want to make some kind of payment on what Robbie owes us?"

And then all movement seemed to stop.

"I wouldn't."

Her hair went limp at Rafe's low-pitched warning. Marco's breath caught on a shocked gasp and Josie turned to see Rafe standing behind him, his gun pointing to the back of Marco's skull.

"Drop it."

For a few milliseconds, all Josie could hear was Rafe's labored breathing. All she could see was the deadly intent in his dark eyes. The rock-steady hand. And the gun.

Then the knife clattered to the pavement. Rafe swung his free arm around and pointed to the handcuffed man who was struggling to sit up. "Don't even think about it."

And then Robbie's knees buckled and Josie turned all her attention to locking her legs and steadying him against the wall until his wooziness passed and she could walk him to the door.

Jake Lonergan materialized in the doorway, and quickly shifted to grab Robbie's other arm and take the bulk of his weight off her. "I heard the commotion and already called it in," he announced to Rafe. "KCPD's on its way. Is every night at the Shamrock this exciting?"

Josie hesitated to follow the new bartender in. But Robbie was trying to laugh while he bled from a cut in his lip and Rafe was holding two thugs at bay with one gun and some frankly intimidating attitude. The least she could do was to swallow her fear and suspicion and get the injured man inside where she could be of some help.

"Thanks, Jake," she finally answered. "Let's get Robbie to a chair and put some ice on that face."

"Yes, ma'am."

"Josephine." Oh, man, how she hated that name. About as much as she hated seeing the forbidding look that darkened Rafe's handsome face when she met his gaze. "You and I will talk later."

She nodded and hurried ahead of Robbie and Jake to get a towel, some ice and a bottle of whiskey. It would be basic first aid. But Robbie would be all right. Rafe had saved him from something far worse than a beating. His quick reactions and specialized training had saved them all.

And in the process, the tender, vulnerable man who'd opened up to her and the baby a few minutes ago in Robbie's office, had vanished.

"YES, SIR, IT'S all under control here," Rafe reported to his captain, Michael Cutler, over the phone. He switched his cell to the other ear and turned to watch the uniformed officers taking Sammy and Marco away in handcuffs. "If you wouldn't mind, call Trip, Alex and Randy and tell them to head back home. I appreciate you guys being on the alert to back me up with Josie's protection. But this is something else. It's not related to the RGK."

"Do you need anything else from us?" the captain asked. "You know we all have a personal stake in getting that serial killer off the streets. And if protecting Josie will do it, you say the word and we're there."

The flashing strobe of red, white and blue lights finally died as the black and whites cleared the parking lot and took the two thugs up to Fourth Precinct headquarters for bookings on assault and various other offenses. Lingering frissons of adrenaline and his frustration over the foolish risk Josie had taken by disobeying his command to stay put inside were the only things keeping his bruised body standing at this point.

He checked his watch and headed for the Shamrock's back door. "Well, sir, in about three hours I'll have been up twenty-four straight with a false bomb threat and a beat down in between. Once I get Josie back to my apartment, I'm gonna crash hard. Can I get somebody to set up watch outside my building for about eight hours?"

If Cutler okayed the request, then Rafe knew he could drop his guard for a few hours and that Josie would still be well-protected. A shuffle of movement in the background gave him his answer before his commanding officer spoke. "I'm on my way over there now to take first watch. Jillian's out of town at a PT conference and it's hard to sleep without her here, anyway. I'll notify the others so that your place is covered around the clock."

"Thanks." Rafe stopped to inspect the impromptu repair job Jake had done on the back door's busted window. The man did good work. He wasn't ready to give a man he'd just met today his complete trust, but they'd been lucky to have him around tonight. "I'll check in again at ten hundred hours tomorrow."

"Put down your badge for a few hours, Sarge," the captain ordered in that friendly voice of experience tone of his. "Go take care of Josie. And take care of yourself. You're no good to any of us if you're running on fumes. Good night."

"Good night, sir."

More certain of the backup from SWAT One than he was of Captain Cutler's personal advice, Rafe hung up and headed for the sharp voices coming from Robbie's office.

"Ow!" Robbie whined. "You're doing that on purpose, girlie. It stings."

"It's your own fault. Stupid loan sharks. You're about all I have left, Robbie." Her voice was husky, as if she'd been crying—or arguing. Or both. "Get some help before I lose you, too."

The plea in her tone quickened Rafe's pace. He walked in to find Josie dabbing some ointment on his split lip and urging him to keep a cold compress over the eye that had swollen shut. "Is everything okay?" Rafe asked.

He spoke to Robbie, but his gaze was drawn to Josie's weary posture and the fist she kept rubbing at the small of her back as she packed up the first-aid kit. "The patient will live."

"We'll see about that," Robbie protested, finally holding the compress without her help. "I think Nurse Pain here needs to retake the course on bedside manner."

"I'm inclined to let the torture continue if it'll knock some sense into you." Rafe grabbed a chair from against the wall and set it beside the desk so that Josie could sit while she fussed over her uncle. "How much do you owe this time?"

"Eight large."

· "Eight thousand?"

"I just made a down payment with all the bar's profits from this weekend and tonight. But by the time I get the rest of what I owe, their interest will have doubled the price."

"At least that explains where the money went," Josie groused. "Those men could have killed you."

Robbie slowly shook his head. "Can't get money from a dead man."

She caught his thick-fingered hand and squeezed. "Not funny. What if Rafe had gotten hurt rescuing you? Or…" She glanced toward Rafe without quite meeting his gaze. "Or the baby?"

"What if Josie had gotten hurt?" Rafe pointed out. He didn't know how much Josie had told her uncle about the identity of the killer she'd seen visiting Patrick, but whether the threat came from the RGK or a pair of leg breakers, she'd put herself at risk tonight. "She was out in the open. I was a little preoccupied. You were down. If somebody wanted to hurt her, she'd have been an easy target tonight."

"Ah, girlie." Robbie lowered the compress and leaned forward in his chair. "I'd never let you or the wee one be hurt. I'm sorry. It's me own mess. I'll get meself out of it as quick as I can." He pressed a kiss to the top of her head as he stood. "Don't you worry your pretty head about me. Tomorrow, I'll look in the phone book for one of those Gamblers Anonymous meetings."

"Do it tonight." She stood to give him a hug. "I love you, you old fool."

"I'm not quite the hero your father was, am I?"

Josie pulled away, her pretty face marred by a frown.

"Dad wasn't perfect. None of us is. He always looked up to you, and was glad you brought him to the States. He'd be the first one to say you can beat this gambling addiction. That's one thing we Nicholses have plenty of…" She glanced back at Rafe, reminding him of the conversation that had been interrupted earlier. "…stubbornness."

"I wish I had your faith, Josie." Robbie picked up the whiskey she'd been using for medicinal purposes and headed toward his apartment upstairs. He paused for a moment in the doorway and asked for a favor. "Take care of our girl, Sergeant."

"I will."

When the door had closed behind her uncle, Josie hurried around the desk. "Rafe, do something."

If he'd been thinking she'd want to resume that conversation about the baby, he'd been mistaken. "Like what? Give him the money? I can pay off his debt, but if he doesn't get help with his addiction, he'll get into trouble somewhere else." He could handle daggers better than the despair that was coming from those big blue eyes. "Those two who tried to shake him down for the money aren't talking, but I'm guessing they're already on the vice squad's radar. I'm guessing Robbie is, too."

Had the circles beneath her eyes been that noticeable before? "You think KCPD is watching Robbie? What do they suspect him of?"

"Probably nothing." He held up his hands, hoping to placate her distress and get her to sit again before she collapsed. "But I'm sure they're thinking that someone who drops that much money every month can lead them to the lowlifes like Thug One and Thug Two back there that they *are* trying to catch."

"Tell them to stop, or it'll be like Patrick all over again." So calming and sitting was a no-go. "My family has sacrificed too much already. I've lost a father and a brother to crime." In one jerky movement, she choked back a sob and grabbed at the small of her back. "I won't lose the only family I have left."

"Honey, I can't tell vice squad what to do." Oh, man, she was hurting—physically and emotionally. Rafe inched forward, wanting to ease her pain, yet needing her to see the sense in what he was saying. He understood the dysfunction of a fractured family, and had learned long ago, that sometimes, love and wishing it so just wasn't enough to make one come together again. "We tried to keep Patrick away from the drugs and dealing. Hard talks. Consequences. Intervention. Failed rehabs. Both of us know Patrick was the only one who could save himself from the road he was on."

She gripped the corner of the desk as she sniffed back the next sob. "You've butted in and taken over my life, trying to fix everything that's wrong with it. Why don't you butt in and fix Robbie's problems, too?"

Butting in? He was trying to do the right thing here. Trying to keep her safe. Trying to keep a promise.

The first tears spilled over and he knew she was physically and emotionally exhausted.

Take care of Josie. Whether the order came from her father or Captain Cutler—or that well-guarded cache of emotions inside him—it was one he would always follow.

"Hey. Shh." Despite a token protest, Rafe pulled

Josie away from the desk and into his arms. With her forehead brushing against his collar, and her elbows wedged between them, she trembled on her feet and her tears ran in stilted, noisy sobs. He reached behind her to loosen the band holding her hair up so tightly, then sifted the weight of the sable waves through his fingers. "You've got more than Robbie in your corner. Remember that. I'll do what I can to protect him. I'll keep him safe. I'll keep all of you safe."

"But—"

"Shh." He recalled her words from that night in the truck, and perhaps, tonight, he was just beginning to understand what she'd meant. "That's how it is in a relationship. Sometimes, one half needs more than the other at a given time."

"But we're not in a relation... Uh."

He dropped his other hand down to the small of her back and gently kneaded his fingers into the knot of muscles there. Josie gasped in pain and tensed against him, her fingers fisting in the front of his starched, dusty shirt. But he kept massaging until the tension eased and she went limp against him.

They stood like that for countless minutes, with Josie's curved body snugged against his. Her tears quieted into a steady rhythm, soaked through his T-shirt to warm his skin, and then ceased altogether.

"Who are you, and what have you done with Rafael Delgado?" She shifted her stance to wind her arms around his waist and nestled closer. "I thought I was getting a lecture."

"You are."

He leaned back to cup her face and tilt it up to his.

Her eyes widened, then drifted shut as he dipped his mouth to kiss her forehead. He gently kissed each eyelid, easing the fever there. Then he moved lower, supping up the salty tracks of her tears over her cheeks and jaw. And then he hovered over the decadent fullness of her unadorned lips, letting his breath caress her mouth, feeling her breath tickling across his skin. He waited until her eyes fluttered open, denying himself what he wanted most until he saw the light of acceptance, of welcome, of answering need in her eyes.

Josie anchored her hands on his shoulders and rose up on her toes to meet him halfway before he closed his mouth over hers with a hungry claim. Her soft lips parted beneath his and he plunged his tongue inside to find hers waiting, daring him to dance along with hers. Rafe kissed her hard, kissed her softly. He lapped up the remnants of her tears and offered comfort, strength, desire. Whatever she needed, it was hers for the taking.

And what he needed… Oh, what he needed. Every foray of her tongue, every press of her lips, every needy grasp of her fingertips against his skin—he absorbed it like a blessing. He fed on the gift of her passion, let her inside the shield of his soul, filled himself up with the need to love this woman and be loved by her.

But he could lose her. He could lose so much if he ever let Josie Nichols too far inside him.

He wasn't the man she thought he was. He didn't know about kids, didn't know about real relationships. He was over six feet tall, knew more about guns and bombs and violence than most people knew about the TV shows they watched. He'd killed men, put down threats, faced danger every damn day of his life.

Yet he was afraid of this beautiful pregnant woman. He was afraid of Aaron Nichols's daughter. He was afraid to really, truly love her.

Because love meant pain.

Love was believing his father wouldn't knock him out cold if he crossed his path on a drunken rampage. Love was believing the apology after strips of skin had been flayed from his back.

Love was believing a fiancée would understand his commitment to his work and support him for who he was instead of humiliating him at the altar.

Love was a brave little boy, dying in his arms—believing Rafe could save him.

Love was believing.

And after thirty-four years of love like that, he just couldn't believe anymore.

His screwed-up self would be a hell of a burden for any woman. And he would never be that burden to Josie.

So he ended the kiss. He tore his mouth from hers and rubbed his cheek against her silky hair, crushing her in a hug until he could stop up the emotions she inevitably unleashed inside him.

Once he eased his grip and her heels sank to the floor, he felt Josie smile against his neck. "I like this new style of lecturing, Rafe."

Oh, yeah, that.

He eased her back and cupped her face again. Something inside him got stuck out of place and refused to completely shut down the emotions that still hummed at the sight of her trusting eyes and beautifully pinkened, kiss-stung lips.

"Don't you ever, ever put yourself into the middle of something like that again. Understand? I'm not just trying to protect you from a killer—I'm trying to protect you, period."

With a nod, she freed herself from his hands and snuggled against his chest again. He tried to distance himself, tried to keep his hands off her, but he lost the battle. "We need you, Rafe. I thought I could do this alone, but I can't. We need you."

He folded his arms around her and rested his cheek against the crown of her hair, feeling a possessive sense of rightness and that seductive calm that filled him when Josie Nichols got around the barriers he tried to keep in place.

THE MAN SET his camera in his lap to watch the black pickup truck drive away from the Shamrock Bar's parking lot.

The light from the upstairs apartment had gone out half an hour ago. So what had the stern-faced cop and Josie Nichols been doing for thirty minutes? Sitting in his vehicle in the dark, with his telephoto lens mounted on his camera, he'd had plenty of time to think about the answer.

Plenty of time to decide how to silence Josie Nichols before he left town. He hated that a woman had been the one to see him kill Kyle Austin that day. His blood pulsed with a familiar heat. He hated that a woman had any kind of power over him. *He* controlled his own destiny, not a woman. *He* would decide where he went and what he did and who he loved, not some woman.

Since the last beating he'd taken as a teenager, when

his father and uncles had abandoned him at a hospital and severed all ties with him, he'd been his own man. He'd changed his name, changed his face, and changed how he dealt with the people who interfered with what he wanted and deserved.

For all his family knew, he was dead. And so was the boy who had been Donny Kemp. He'd taken all he'd learned from his grifter family—how to charm, how to deceive, how to plan, how to punish anyone who muffed up the con—and had transformed himself into someone who would never allow anyone to control him again. No woman would take his job, refuse his heart or turn him over to the police to join his father and uncles in prison.

He'd been successful for years, meting out justice, righting the balance in his world.

He'd been successful until last year, when he'd run up against the black-suited warriors of KCPD's SWAT Team One. They'd volunteered as bodyguards, shielding the women who'd wronged him so badly.

Despite the balmy, late-night air flowing through the open windows of his vehicle, he shivered. There was too much rage trapped inside him, too much satisfaction he'd been denied.

What was it with these SWAT cops, anyway? They'd already interfered with dispatching two of his intended victims. Two women who'd taken what was rightfully his, who'd looked down their arrogant noses at him without ever really seeing him. These SWAT men in black, with all their guns and expertise and heroics, had come between him and the women he was compelled to destroy. And now there was a third cop, watching over Josie Nichols.

He reached for a cigarette to calm his nerves. It was a dirty, smelly habit, and he loathed the stench that lingered on his clothes. But clothes could be washed or pitched, and the nicotine calmed him, allowed him to think clearly. With this particular neighborhood of downtown Kansas City shut down for the night, and the parking lot abandoned, there'd be no one to see the flare of his lighter. He inhaled a deep breath and blew the smoke out into the dampish air.

This cop guarding Josie Nichols was different from the other two SWAT cops who'd thwarted him, though. This one, with his surly moods and fearlessness for confrontation, seemed a lot like him. The way he'd shown no mercy to the first mugger, slamming him down to the asphalt and handcuffing him into submission, the way he'd pulled his gun on the man with the knife who'd gone after Josie, reminded him of skills he possessed. As he'd watched through the lens of his camera, he'd had no doubt that this cop would have pulled the trigger without batting an eye.

While he understood the cop, his refusal to leave Josie's side presented a problem. With his other victims, there'd been social events he could use to his advantage to gain access to them. And while getting into a bar, even the Shamrock, had never been a challenge for him, the unique clientele of this particular one meant he'd have to find another way to get to her.

His fingers tightened convulsively around the camera in his lap, then relaxed as the answer came to him.

Pulling out the ashtray, he put out the cigarette, carefully smushing it down to the same height as the other two butts beside it. Then he turned on the camera and scrolled through the pictures on the memory card. He clicked past the picture of the SWAT cop holding the Glock 9 mm to the attacker's head. He clicked past the image of the bruiser with the knife clutching Josie's hair. There. That was his answer. He smiled and felt the tension inside him relax a bit.

He smiled at the image of Josie Nichols kneeling beside her bloodied uncle—her face frightened, her hand clutched at her swollen belly, her mouth open, pleading, shouting for the violence to stop.

The fat man's troubles could work to his advantage. She cared about her brother in prison and she cared about Robbie Nichols. Both would be easier to get to than the woman, and that could draw her out and into his net.

If he couldn't get to Josie through that cop who seemed to always be around her, then maybe he could get to her in another way. He could get to the things she loved.

He turned off the camera and quickly disassembled it, packing the lens and camera into the appropriate compartments of his carrying case. He set the case on the passenger-side floorboard and squared the rectangular bag up between the edges of the seat and dashboard. Finally, he started the car and pulled out onto the street. He cruised past the garish green neon shamrock hanging inside the bar's front window before turning on his lights and merging into the three o'clock, morning traffic.

He wanted to get his hands around Josie Nichols's throat—he needed to have her dead.

And if someone else had to suffer in order to make that happen, well, he had no problem with that.

Chapter Eight

The following Saturday had begun like every other
day that week.

Josie would try to sleep in Rafe's bed and wind up
dozing in fits and starts while she stayed at his apartment, partly because she felt so guilty for kicking the
man out of his own bed and relegating him to the living
room couch, and partly because the crisp cotton sheets
and pillows where she'd rested the last four nights had
teased her with his scent and felt inexplicably cold
despite the blanket spread on top. She'd awakened
each morning to the sounds of Rafe moving about the
kitchen, starting his pot of coffee, heating some water
for her decaffeinated tea. Then, while he showered and
dressed, Josie cooked some eggs and toast. They'd sit
down at opposite ends of his kitchen table and go over
their schedule for the day while they ate.

Rafe wasn't the chattiest of company. But in a way,
she liked that. The companionable silence gave her a
chance to fully wake up and get her game face on for the
day. When breakfast was done, she'd get in the shower
while he cleaned the kitchen. Their routine could have
been the real domestic bliss she'd always fantasized
about.

Except for the bliss part.

Like that kiss in Robbie's office after the attack on Monday night.

That embrace had been crazy, unexpected, wonderful. When she'd been expecting another stern reminder about taking unnecessary risks for others and not listening to him and endangering herself because she'd agreed to look at the face of a serial killer, she'd gotten the best massage of her life, an earth-tilting kiss and a glimpse into the heart of Rafe Delgado.

That was bliss.

Being cared for. Wanted. Feeling so necessary to someone's existence that there was no place for the loneliness inside her.

But that had been a late-night kiss and a supportive hug after a harrowing event. Apparently, this was the bliss-free reality she needed to get used to.

Somehow, even though Rafe was considerate of her needs and always seemed to be around, she felt almost farther apart than ever. It was as though that kiss in Robbie's office, which had turned her inside out with its slow, driving sensuality and raw honesty, had tapped out all of Rafe's emotions. A barrier had been breached that night, touching something that went even deeper than the night they'd made love in his truck. And now Rafe was shoring up his defenses. He was almost sweeter, less moody than before the kiss. But it was a shell of Rafael Delgado, a facade.

And she missed the man whose passions and convictions and deepest scars filled up a room and made him volatile and courageous and more fiercely caring than even he knew he could be.

Other than the fact that they were living together for protection purposes, she loved the man more than ever and he wouldn't allow himself to care about her the way Josie knew he could, it was business as usual.

Although the location was a little different, reporting to this morning's meeting at the Fourth Precinct conference room to meet with the event planners in charge of the staff for KCPD's Spring Carnival fundraiser was like any other of the odd jobs she often took to make ends meet. Only Rafe was lurking in the building somewhere, waiting for the orientation to finish. And pretty much every cop who'd known her father had stopped her to say hi, congratulate her on the baby, and ask her who the lucky daddy was.

Did Rafe want anyone to know he was Junior's father? Or was that another secret she'd be forced to hide away right alongside the love he didn't seem to want?

Jeffrey Beecher, the assistant to Clarice Darnell, the platinum blonde speaking at the podium, came by Josie's table and set a sheaf of papers on top of the tax form in front of her. That he stopped long enough to straighten the stack of handouts for her pulled Josie's attention back to the red-lacquered fingernails dancing in the air as Ms. Darnell emphasized the point she was making.

"Of course, with new security regulations, everyone working the event will need to be screened," Ms. Darnell explained. "Now all of you have worked with us before or have come highly recommended to us by other agencies. Still, since this is a police-sponsored event, we're requiring two forms of ID. Your driver's license and a student ID card or work permit, or even a copy of your local utility bill, will work. Rest assured, none of this information will be disseminated beyond my immediate staff and the KCPD. Make sure you meet with Jeffrey and get a copy made before you leave today." Clarice pointed to her assistant, who held up his hand and waved to the thirty or so men and women their firm was hiring for the event. "The second form is a health affidavit we're asking everyone to…"

Josie picked up the papers to find the form Clarice had referred to, but ended up knocking one to the floor as she sorted through them. With a weary sigh, she scooted to the edge of the chair and adjusted her belly between her thighs so she could lean over and pick it up.

But another hand reached it first. "Allow me."

The man sitting closest to her, "Bud," according to the name embroidered on his gray canvas uniform jacket, scooped the paper up. He leaned over the chair between them, giving her a good whiff of the cigarette smoke clinging to his clothes, as he returned the paper to her. "Are you going to be able to handle this workload, darlin'?" he whispered, his gaze dropping to the bump thrusting against the cotton of her hospital scrubs.

Although the acrid smell radiating from him tickled her nose and made her stomach do a queasy little roll, Josie appreciated the help. "Thanks."

Bud turned his face back to the speaker, but leaned in her direction and continued the hushed conversation. "I'd be happy to stick close and do any heavy lifting you might need done."

Josie rubbed her belly and whispered back. "I'm pregnant, not an invalid. I've always been able to handle the job I was hired to do."

"Ah, an independent woman. Single mama, I bet. I'm just sayin' it's good to look out for each other, right?" She'd hoped a nod to the front of the room would encourage him to refocus his attention, but now he was pointing out her scrubs. "You work at a hospital?"

"I'm a nursing student. I'll get my R.N. degree at the end of the summer."

"So this menial kind of work is beneath you. It's just how you pay for the important stuff."

Josie bristled at the idea that she, of all people, might be looked at as a snob. "I've never been afraid of hard work."

"Then let's make it a tradeoff. Because I think you and I could be friends." When he turned to face her, she saw he had a toothpick that he kept teasing with his tongue tucked into the corner of his mouth. Her stomach roiled in response to the suggestive movement. "I'll carry anything heavy for you at this shindig, and if I cut myself, you can stitch me up and kiss my boo-boo—"

"Bud. I need you to stop flirting and pay attention." Josie was grateful for Jeffrey Beecher's hushed tone of authority.

"Was I flirtin'?" Bud asked innocently, looking to the end of the table where Jeffrey stood. "I thought I was being polite to the little lady."

This guy was just too weird. And though it was impossible to gauge his height when they were sitting, she couldn't get a good look at his face to see if he reminded her in any way of the man in the hospital parking lot or the killer she'd seen in the prison visitation room. His short, thinning brown hair could easily be masked by a ball cap or a bad toupee. She pulled her gaze from the gross distraction of the toothpick and focused in on his eyes. Were they cold? Colorless?

"You and I can talk later when the boss isn't—"

"Bud." Jeffrey Beecher's sharp tone turned Bud's face away and ended the opportunity to make a definitive match to the RGK.

Maybe, like she'd suspected of the good Samaritan who'd disappeared after her car had been sabotaged, Bud was just another random creepy guy. Or maybe, she hated to think, she was going to read threats into every conversation she had with strangers who showed a special interest in her.

Still, as she scooted her chair back in, she also moved a little extra distance between them. She turned to Jeffrey Beecher, who was adjusting his narrow, wire-framed glasses on his nose, and mouthed a "Thank you."

She couldn't see his eyes with the glare of the overhead lights reflecting off the lenses. But she got the idea from the momentary crinkle in his cheek that he'd winked.

Another form and two site maps later—one for Swope Park and another for a nearby convention center in case the weather for the carnival didn't cooperate—plus a long wait to get her IDs approved for working the event, and Josie was finally done with the meeting.

"Remember," Clarice Darnell gave them one last bit of direction before Josie and the other wait staff were dismissed, "we're doing this for the KCPD Widows & Orphans Fund. So look your best and be your friendliest. We want to raise a lot of money for them."

While others lingered to get reacquainted or introduce themselves to new coworkers, Josie booked it out of the conference room. She had about thirty minutes to find a restroom and get herself to the south end of the city and her shift at the Truman Medical Center.

She'd barely cleared the corner when she ran into Spencer Montgomery. Even on a Saturday morning, when most detectives were off the clock or in casual dress, the red-haired detective was wearing his usual impeccable suit and tie. The frown of confusion he wore was less familiar.

Saying a quick prayer that her bladder muscles were stronger than the weight of the baby pressing down on them, she let the detective take her by the arm and guide her into an empty hallway. "What are you doing here?" he asked. "Are you looking for me?"

Josie shook her head. "I'm working at the KCPD fundraiser next Saturday. Since you guys are running security screenings on all of us, Ms. Darnell and Mr. Beecher had us meet here."

"Security screenings?"

"You know, to make sure the city isn't hiring any terrorists or illegals, I suppose."

He glanced toward the conference room and the people still milling about inside. "I'd better pull your info—control who has access to your personal information."

"Won't that send up a red flag that I'm involved in your case?"

When Montgomery faced her again, she could see he had the faintest dusting of freckles across his skin. "I can be discreet," he promised. "And everything else is going all right? Delgado informed me about the man at the hospital and the phone call. Have there been any other incidents?"

"Two men assaulted my uncle at the bar, but that was related to some trouble he got into with a loan shark. Other than suspecting almost every man I meet, no, I don't think I've been accosted by the RGK." She squinched her face into a frown. "At least I don't think I have. I mean, I'll recognize him when I see him again, won't I?"

"You tell me."

Either Junior and her bladder or her own self doubts and weeks of stress were making her antsy. "Sometimes, I think it's been so long that I won't know him when I see him—that maybe I won't know him at all, and it'll be too late before I figure it out."

Detective Montgomery pulled back the front of his jacket, exposing his gun and his badge as he slid his hands into the pockets of his slacks. "Don't let it be too late, Josie. I'm counting on you to ID this bastard. All of Kansas City is."

No pressure, right? Josie tipped her chin up at what sounded like a reprimand. "It's your job to find this guy, right? And then I just look at him from behind a one-way mirror and tell you yes or no?" Her hands moved over her belly in an instinctively protective stance. "You promised to keep my name out of it, right? I have a baby to protect. You wouldn't leak any information about me to smoke him out, would you?"

"Of course not." Some of the chill left his expression. The man could be handsome in a polished sort of way if he ever smiled. "I'm just eager to put this case to bed, and was worried to see you here. I thought Delgado was running security for you."

"He is."

"Then why did he let you out of his sight?"

A tall, dark shadow walked up behind Montgomery. "He didn't."

Rafe was dressed casually today in jeans and a black shirt. But with his badge hanging around his neck, his gun holstered to his belt and his wary scowl locked firmly into place, he looked as intimidating as he did in full SWAT gear.

Josie was happy to see him, although a little surprised to have him drop his arm around her shoulders and claim a connection to her. "Montgomery."

"Delgado," the detective acknowledged without batting an eye. "I don't know if letting Miss Nichols work at an event with as many people in attendance as the KCPD Carnival will have is a good idea."

"I know it isn't."

"Then why allow—?"

"Hey. First of all, no one *lets* me do anything," Josie interrupted, pushing Rafe's arm away. "I make my own decisions. I'm responsible for my own actions. And one of them is earning a living." She would not be treated like she was fifteen and still Daddy's little girl. Nor would she let either of these men make her afraid. "I don't have the luxury of going on vacation or sitting in a secluded safe house while you find this killer who's eluded the authorities for two years now. You both promised to keep me anonymous and safe. I'm depending on that. Now if you'll excuse me, I have to find the bathroom."

Rafe and the red-haired detective both turned to watch her march in her waddling gait down the hall.

She heard Spencer Montgomery ask, "So is she tough enough to see this investigation all the way through to the end?"

"Tough?" She wondered at the humor that colored Rafe's answer. "You have no idea."

"JOSIE!" ROBBIE SHOUTED over the din of the bar's Saturday night crowd. "Telephone!"

"Who the...? Here you go." Josie set the rum and cola she'd just poured on the bar and took the customer's money. "Can you take a message?" she asked, making change at the cash register. "Robbie?"

But he'd already set down the receiver near the coffeepot at the back of the bar and returned to the line of patrons waiting to place their orders. His black eye and bruised mouth couldn't hide his jovial greetings for old friends. He was busy shaking hands, pouring drinks, doing the kind of personal interaction that made the Shamrock such a success.

And, with a huge debt hanging over his head, he needed the bar to continue to thrive. Even though he'd already been to his first two GA meetings, Josie couldn't help but double-check that there was no money changing hands on those handshakes, no sly asides about sure things at the track or what slots were running hot at one of the local casinos.

With a sigh, she wiped her hands on her apron and

picked up the phone. Satisfied that she could let Robbie safely out of her sight for a few seconds, she pulled the cord through the swinging door to take the call in the hallway where the noise from the main room was slightly muted.

She even gave herself permission to sink back against the wall and close her eyes for a few seconds before putting the receiver to her ear. "Hello?"

"Miss me, Josie?" Her eyes popped open and she pushed away from the wall as a familiar voice greeted her with an eerie charm. "I bet you thought I'd forgotten about you."

"How did you get this number?" Josie latched on to the wall as her world started to sway.

"Please, it's in the phone book." He laughed as if it was mere child's play to find her name, where she worked, track her down and terrorize her. "I don't want you to think you and the baby are safe. I've just been busy. Coming up with a plan, along with several contingencies. Watching you."

"Watching?" Josie cupped her hand over her belly and looked up and down the back hallway. She was alone, wasn't she? Her thoughts raced as panic tried to get inside her head. Robbie's office was dark. The door to the walk-in refrigerator was shut. The back door window had been replaced; the door was closed.

But how could she be certain it was locked from here? She stretched the telephone cord taut, but she couldn't reach the door's push bar to check. She jerked her gaze back to Robbie's office. What if someone was lurking in the shadows there? Her pulse was pounding now, throbbing beneath her collar. Where was Jake

Lonergan? The man hadn't said ten words to her since she'd introduced herself last weekend. And he had a penchant for ball caps and hiding his eyes, just like the vanishing man at the hospital.

"Josie." The voice on the phone made a tutting sound, as if any concern he felt for her was real. "I can hear you breathing harder, faster."

"Shut up," she said. He laughed. She inched her way back to the wall, toward the noise from the bar. "You don't scare me," she lied with a bravado she didn't feel. "I've seen your face. I told the police everything about you."

"That's not a very nice way to speak to me." His tone changed, losing its mocking politeness. It deepened, grew impatient. "I know you're alone in the back hallway, you stupid woman. You should be nicer when it's just you and me. And the baby."

The blood froze in Josie's veins. "What?"

He was here.

Watching. *I know you're alone.*

"Now that's an idea." The burst of temper had passed. The cool tones that followed were even more disturbing. "I could ensure your cooperation permanently if I took the baby from you. You'd do whatever I say then, wouldn't you? I wouldn't have to sully my hands around your throat."

You're not alone.

Rafe.

Suddenly, her heart pumped with a vengeance, pouring energy into every limb, clearing a path through the fear. She pushed open the swinging door to the assault of sound and lights inside the bar. She looked past Robbie's broad back and searched the entire bar. Tables were full. Every bar stool was taken. Robbie and Enrico were filling drinks. There were so many people, so many faces. Her eyes went to every ball cap, searched out every face.

Spencer Montgomery and his partner were nowhere to be seen. People were calling out drink orders, shooting pool, flirting with the waitresses, laughing. And she still hadn't spotted Jake Lonergan.

Or those eyes.

Her gaze stopped on every man who held a phone to his ear. Where was he? Who was watching her?

And then, a tunnel cleared through all the chaos and she locked on to a pair of warm, whiskey-brown eyes. Rafe stood at the table where the rest of SWAT Team One sat. He was watching her, reading her distress. The panther-like energy in him furled up, then uncoiled as he strode across the room. His eyes never left hers and she began to shake. From fear? Anticipation? Relief? Rafe nudged aside a waitress at the end of the bar, braced his hand on either side of the station and vaulted over the top of the bar.

Surprised comments and shouts of concern faded into white noise as the voice whispered its vile threats in her ear. "…is too much fun. But I'm waiting for the right moment. It will come. I promise you, it's only a matter of time before I—"

Rafe snatched the receiver from her hand. "Who the hell is this?" he demanded. His arm circled around her and tucked her against the unyielding strength of his body. "You coward. You can't get to her, understand? You show your face and…damn it." Josie heard the click herself as the caller disconnected. Rafe hung up the phone, spared half a second to assess their surroundings, then pushed open the swinging door and pulled her into the quiet of the hallway with him.

Josie instinctively pushed away. "No. He said he could see me back here."

"Shh. You're safe." She could feel Rafe moving, turning, no doubt peering into every nook and shadow, even as he overpowered her stiff arms and pulled her into his chest. The fear and panic whooshed out in a breathy sigh that left her knees weak and Josie willingly leaned against him, curling her fingers into the starchy crispness of his black cotton shirt. On duty or off, the man radiated an abundance of heat that beckoned her to align her misshapen body tightly against his to absorb the energy and comfort he offered. Rafe didn't seem to mind, palming the back of her head and turning her cheek into the V of skin at the open collar of his shirt. Josie wound her arms around his waist and nestled beneath his chin. "You're safe."

But the reprieve was far too short. The door swung open again and again, startling her each time until she gave up her haven and turned to face the men filing into the hallway.

"Sarge?"

"Is she all right?"

"What's up?"

"Talk to me."

In a matter of seconds, Josie was surrounded by her Uncle Robbie and the circle of SWAT Team One.

"What the hell is going on here?" Robbie protested. "Jumping over me bar like some kind of—"

Rafe raised his head and her uncle fell silent.

For a moment. Then Robbie's thick fingers lightly tapped her arm. "Girlie, what's wrong?"

But Rafe's captain, Michael Cutler, knew. "The RGK?"

Rafe nodded. "He called her again. Now that he can't get to her at her apartment, he's harassing her here."

"RGK?" Robbie repeated. "The Rich Girl Killer? The man in all the papers? What does Josie have to do with all that?"

Rafe dropped his arm behind her back, linking her to him, looking down over the jut of his shoulder at her. "What did he say to you?"

"That he's watching me." Josie tipped her head back to meet his shrouded gaze, then turned to include the others. "He knew I was alone in the back hallway."

Rafe's fingers pinched the side of her waist as he slipped into SWAT cop mode. He pointed to Alex Taylor and Randy Murdock, gesturing them toward the back door. "Fan out. I want this building searched roof to cellar, inside and out." Then he looked up at Trip Jones. One by one, they were all checking guns, moving their badges to visible locations at their waist or shirt pocket. "We need to shut this bar down."

"On a Saturday night?" Robbie protested. Josie's hands slid down to hug her belly through her apron and jeans, trembling at the sounds and sights of the four men and one woman going to war—for her. Robbie put up his hands and surrendered. "I'll announce last call. Make up some excuse. I don't want any harm coming to me girl."

"Go," Rafe ordered.

Trip grabbed Robbie's shoulder, silently promising to explain everything later. "I can clear a room." He caught the door before following Robbie through. "You want me to recruit some help in the search out there?"

"No. Until we put a face on this guy, I don't know who to trust." The snap in Rafe's voice made his meaning clear. He trusted his SWAT team—but everyone else was suspect.

Trip read the message loud and clear, too, giving Rafe a nod. "I'll take care of it."

Rafe finally turned to the tall, authoritative man with the shots of silver in his coal black hair. "Sorry, sir. I didn't mean to overstep my authority by giving orders. I know we're off the clock." His hand slid over to pull Josie's from her stomach and lace their fingers together between them. "I just reacted to the situation. I should have let you—"

"We're here to keep an eye on her, Sarge, so no apology needed." Captain Cutler's blue eyes reflected the respect Rafe clearly felt. "This is your op. We've all stepped up when something dangerous hits close to home. As I recall, you totaled your last truck to save Alex Taylor's life when we first got involved with this RGK mess."

"Taylor and his fiancée's lives are worth a lot more than a truck."

"That's my point. Don't think that any one of us would do any less for you." His dark eyes warmed as he nodded to Josie, and then he was all business again when he turned to Rafe. "Now what do you need from me?"

"This is Montgomery's case." Rafe's hand tightened

around hers. "The RGK makes a move the one night he isn't around pressing Josie for answers. We need to fill him in on the latest threat and get him here."

"Done. I'll start a search upstairs while I'm at it." Rafe's commanding officer pulled out his cell phone and punched in a number as he strode down the hall. "Dispatch. This is Captain Cutler, SWAT Team One. Put me through to Detective Spencer Montgomery."

Josie's shell-shocked emotions shivered back to life as the captain left and the shadows of the bar's back hallway closed in on her. She was fearful that one of Rafe's friends would get hurt helping her—angry that there was some loathsome, resourceful, homicidal stalker out there who made these good people have to take up arms in the first place. The smells of spilled alcohol and polished wood, the echoes of protesting customers and curious questions drifted in from the bar, then faded out again when Rafe pressed a kiss to her temple and tugged on her hand to pull her into step beside him.

"Come on. You're shaking like a leaf. Let's go into Robbie's office and get another locked door between you and that bastard."

Rafe flipped on the light and scanned the room before closing the door behind them and throwing the dead bolt. Then he led her around the desk and pulled out Robbie's office chair for her to sit while he checked the windows and closed the blinds.

Every movement was precise, every step had purpose. He was tall and masculine, armed, focused... Josie's topsy-turvy hormones jumped in a decidedly female response to the man who'd leaped to her aid after a single look. Something equally potent stirred in her belly. They were tiny pulses of life moving inside her, the life she'd created with this man.

A life that another man had threatened to take.

Josie wound her arms around the precious heartbeat and sank back into the leather chair, her emotional fatigue making her lightheaded.

"Hey." Rafe's sharp eyes didn't miss a trick. "You feeling okay?" He hurried over to the mini-fridge beside the door and pulled out a bottle of water. He knelt in front of her, unscrewing the top and putting the bottle into her hands. "You're not going to pass out on me, are you?"

Shaking her head, she took a sip of water, feeling the cool liquid trickle all the way down her throat. Although the drink revived her a bit, it couldn't penetrate the darkening twist of her thoughts.

Rafe's eyes narrowed, the sun lines beside them evident with his concern. "Jose?"

Josie plucked the lid from his fingers and closed the bottle. She set it on the desk with an ominous thump. "He talked about our baby, Rafe. He said he would use Junior to shut me up."

The timbre of his voice roughened with gravel when he spoke. "It's an idle threat. He's just trying to get under your skin."

"It's working."

With that failed attempt at humor, Rafe pulled her to her feet and into his arms. He slid one hand down to that vulnerable spot at the small of her back and tunneled the other beneath her ponytail to rub the base of her neck. While Josie wound her arms around his waist, he dipped his head and whispered into her ear. "You're tough, Josie Nichols. You work harder than anybody I know, smile more than the world deserves. Hell, you put up with me—you have to be tough." That triggered a wry little laugh and she felt him smiling against her hair. She savored his firm, possessive touch as much as she savored his pep talk. "You can beat this guy. He had no idea what kind of woman he was going up against when he took you on. Aaron would be so proud of you. I'm a little in awe myself."

The sandpapery stubble of beard growth on his neck tickled Josie's lips as they curved with a real smile. "You have your finer moments when you're actually quite…" She swallowed hard and burrowed into his strength. She had to say it. "I love you, Rafe. I know you don't want to hear that, but I do. You've always been there for me—when Dad died, when Patrick needed help and went to prison, now, through all this. You've always been my hero." She brought her hand to rest atop the steady beat of his strong heart. "Just let me say that. I know emotions are hard for you, but that's what I'm feeling. I don't want to drive you away, but I'm tired of lying and pretending they're not there. It's too much work for me to bottle them all up inside. I need you to know that."

She held her breath and counted heartbeats, waiting for him to release her or argue the point. Instead, Rafe leaned back to frame her face between his hands and tilt her gaze up to his. "I'm good at one thing, honey. Being a cop. When I lost Aaron, I lost what little bit of sense the world made for me. I lost Calvin Chambers, and it about killed me inside." His deep breath warmed her cheek. "I am not going to lose you. That's a promise I can make. He's not going to hurt you. Or the baby. I need *you* to know that."

When he wrapped her back in his arms and held her until the members of his team called in with situation reports, Josie didn't protest. He hadn't offered a declaration of love or even an acknowledgment of the relationship that had always existed in the background between them. Maybe those were words she was never going to hear from Rafael Delgado.

But she could believe in his actions, right? She could trust that this good man, who'd been so damaged by life, meant everything he *was* willing to say. For now, if he held her close, if he stood by her and the baby when she was most afraid, it would have to be enough for her lonesome heart.

Chapter Nine

Rafe had never seen Spencer Montgomery in anything other than a suit and tie. Still, at 12:30 a.m., dressed in a dark green polo shirt and jeans, he managed to look clean-shaven, coldhearted, and too arrogant for Rafe's liking as he closed his notebook and tucked it into his back pocket. "You're certain it was Donny Kemp?"

"Who else would threaten me?" Josie threw up her hands, then quickly clutched them back in her lap. "I don't have any enemies."

"You're telling me Josie's involved with a serial killer?" Robbie Nichols circled his office, interrupting the conversation between his niece and the detective who were sitting at his desk.

"Uncle Robbie, please," Josie chided, urging him to stop his pacing. Rafe read the plea in her eyes before turning back to the red-haired detective. "I'm sorry. Is there anything else?"

Rafe stopped Robbie with a look and straightened from the counter where he'd been watching Montgomery's every interaction with Josie. She looked exhausted. Despite her determination to answer every question, clarifying the few details KCPD had on Donny Kemp and his reincarnation as the Rich Girl

Killer, the shadows darkening beneath her eyes worried him. The book he'd been reading said pregnant women needed extra sleep, and he knew from the tossing and sighing he'd heard from his side of the bedroom door that Josie had been getting even less than usual lately.

"There was no distortion to the voice you spoke with on the phone?" Montgomery asked.

Rafe moved at the weary sigh that collapsed Josie's posture. "She's already answered that." He crossed Robbie's office to stand beside her chair and rest a supportive hand on her shoulder. "She should be able to identify the RGK by his vocal patterns as well as his new face. What are you going to do to stop the harassing phone calls?"

Robbie came to the desk, completing a triangle surrounding Josie. "I'll tell you what he should do."

"Sir…" Montgomery stood.

"Robbie," Rafe warned.

"No. Now I'll not have any harm comin' to her here." The older man shook his meaty fist. "I'll be handin' out a little Irish justice if that bastard shows his face at my bar."

Josie pushed to her feet. "Uncle Robbie, enough. I got involved with this to try to keep anyone else from getting hurt. It was just a phone call."

"It was a phone call that turned you white as a ghost and got these fine fellas with their guns and badges all stirred up." He turned his bruised blue eyes to Rafe. "My brother would be rollin' over in his grave if he knew the mess his little girl had gotten herself into."

The accusation was clear, although whether he was referring to the murder or the baby or both wasn't. Rafe didn't back down, however. He was guilty as charged— and determined to make good on the debt he owed this family. "I'll die before he gets his hands on her, I promise."

"Rafe, don't say things like that." Josie's fingers brushed against his forearm.

His skin leaped in response to her touch and he pulled away, needing to retain control of the situation, the room—of every needy impulse—if he intended to do this job right. "You want me to say what I mean."

He had to turn away from the pain in those beautiful blue eyes.

Robbie raked his fingers through his hair, leaving the unruly mop in a mess. "She shouldn't have to deal with this—on top of my troubles, and the baby. And you should have told me straightway, girlie, instead of letting me find out like this. I could have done more to help."

"You can't tell anyone what we've discussed here tonight, Mr. Nichols." Detective Montgomery carried his chair back around to the visitor's side of the desk, probably just as worried about Robbie's garrulous mouth and impulsive nature as Rafe was. "I'll get a tap added to this line at the Shamrock in addition to the one in her apartment. But he hasn't called there for a couple of weeks now. He must know she's not living there." He set the chair down and faced Rafe across the desk. "Any indication the RGK knows she's staying at your place?"

"She's staying with you?" Robbie sounded surprised.

"I've got friends watching her 24/7. There, at the hospital, here."

"So you've got eyes on her. What about the surrounding area?" Rafe bristled at the implication he might not be doing his job right. "The RGK isn't above creating collateral damage to serve as a diversion. Or to draw her out by going after the things and people she cares about."

"You think I don't know that?"

"You're the guy who knocked her up?" Robbie sounded incredulous. "You know better than to—"

"Robbie," Josie warned.

"'Knocked up?'" Rafe's hands curled into fists at the slang term applied to the woman who seemed so proud about carrying a child. So protective of it. "You know better than to talk to her like that."

Detective Montgomery was still making himself a part of the mix, too. "He could be gunning for you, Delgado."

Rafe whirled around. "That's why I've got backup."

"Stop it!" Josie's sharp cry silenced them all. "All of you." She hugged her arms around her middle, turning from one man to the next. "My personal life isn't up for discussion. I've told you everything I know. And you?" Those blue eyes cut right through Rafe. "I just want to leave. Now."

"Jose, I—"

Alex Taylor's compact, muscular figure appeared in the doorway before any of them could make an apology. "Sarge, we've got an unwelcome visitor outside."

Every cell in Rafe's body was being pulled like a magnet to go to Josie, wrap her up in his arms and get her out of here. He checked his watch instead. "I thought we had the place cleared and locked down an hour ago."

"We ran the plates on all the cars left in the lot, and the owners are all accounted for. This guy's not a customer or a cop. You're not gonna like this." Alex arched a dark eyebrow and tossed a plastic card attached to a lanyard to Rafe. "Here are his press credentials."

Rafe caught the laminated identification card and swore when he read the name. "Steve Lassen. Bottomfeeder."

"Unfortunately, he's keeping a legal distance, or I'd have sent him packing already," Alex reported.

Rafe would like nothing better than to turn Alex loose to go after the man who'd once targeted his fiancée. But then he'd have a whole different set of issues to deal with, and Rafe was barely managing the problems he'd already created for himself. "I don't want Josie's face in the papers."

"Let me see that." Detective Montgomery took the card and uttered an expletive to match Rafe's. "Lassen's been following me around since the press conference, sucking up every tidbit of information he can. He's a blot on this city." At least they agreed on one thing. Montgomery crumpled the ID in his fist and moved toward the door. He pointed to Rafe. "You get her out of here. I'll get rid of this guy."

A few minutes later, Rafe shrugged into his leather jacket while he and Robbie waited at the back door for Josie to finish in the bathroom.

"I always counted you among my friends, Rafael." Robbie's Irish temper was still brewing beneath the surface. "But to not do the right thing by our Josie…"

The bathroom door opened and Josie came out, buttoning a sweater over her blouse and shifting her backpack onto her shoulder. "Be nice. Rafe didn't know about the baby. I didn't tell him until this mess with the Rich Girl Killer started."

Rafe didn't expect Josie to defend him, but he was relieved to see the paternal condemnation easing up a bit in Robbie's expression. "I don't understand you young people sometimes." He pulled Josie in for a hug and pressed a noisy kiss on her cheek. "But I love ya." He thumped Rafe on the shoulder before pushing the door open for them. "You keep our girl safe, understand?"

"Yes, sir." Rafe wrapped his fingers around Josie's elbow, scanned the nearly empty parking lot, and waited to spot Michael Cutler leaning against his truck.

The high sign the captain gave him indicated the truck was secure. "I sent Murdock on to your apartment and Trip's keeping an eye on the traffic out front."

With a nod, Rafe stepped out with Josie.

"Hold up!" the captain cautioned, pushing away from the truck.

A light flashed off to the left. "That's her, isn't it?" a man's voice called out. "She's your witness."

Rafe instinctively hunched his shoulders around Josie and pushed her back toward the building. "Captain?"

"Damn it, Lassen!" That was Spencer Montgomery. "I warned you."

Multiple sets of footsteps crunched across the asphalt.

Steve Lassen might have driven away, but he'd snuck

back into the area on foot. Rafe spotted him moving behind a car at the edge of the parking lot, beyond where he'd parked. "She's the one who can bring down the RGK."

"He took my picture." Josie latched on to his sleeve as Rafe braced her in the open doorway. "He can't have my picture."

"What's going on?" Robbie asked, pulling her in beside him.

"Take her." Rafe spun around to see Spencer Montgomery running down the reporter in the neighboring lot.

"I have First Amendment rights!" Lassen protested.

Montgomery caught him and put him down on the pavement. "You just lost them when you violated my order."

"I've got him, Detective." Alex Taylor had joined the chase as well, and in seconds had his knee in Lassen's back. He cuffed Lassen's wrists together while Montgomery pried a camera from his fingers. "Did he get a pic?"

Montgomery was up on his feet, breathing hard and pushing buttons as he looked at the back of the digital camera. "There. I deleted it."

He tossed the camera to the ground.

"Hey, watch it!" Lassen protested. "That equipment costs money."

"So does a lawsuit," Montgomery warned. He pulled the reporter up to his feet and glanced over his shoulder at Rafe. "Get her out of here." He scooped the camera up from beneath the Dumpster and dropped it into his pocket. "I'd like to have a long, private talk with Mr. Lassen."

After Detective Montgomery loaded Lassen into the backseat of his car, and drove away lecturing him about impeding his investigation, Alex Taylor jogged back over to Rafe. "All right, Sarge, let's do this. Captain? Are we clear?"

"Move out."

This time, with guns drawn down at their sides, the three SWAT cops formed a triangle around Josie and walked her out to Rafe's truck.

Robbie Nichols followed behind them, angling over to the car at the edge of the lot where Steve Lassen had been lying in wait. Robbie swore and Josie stumbled, wanting to stop and see what had upset her uncle.

"Who the hell moved my car?"

Odd comment to make. Rafe tightened his arm around Josie's back, drawing her up against his hip to get her moving again. He didn't like *odd*. He slid a look from Alex to Robbie.

Taylor nodded and split from the group. "I'll check it out. Mr. Nichols?"

Robbie was fuming now. "This is Sammy and Marco's doing. Damn loan sharks. You tell your boss I'll pay his freaking debt. You can't intimidate me or me girl."

"Robbie?" Josie squirmed at Rafe's side. His fingers slid against her swollen abdomen, against the baby he'd put there, distracting him for a split second.

A split second too long.

"Hit the deck!" Captain Cutler yelled.

Rafe jerked his head around to catch the flash of light erupting beneath the hood of the car.

"Robbie!"

Alex took the big man down with a flying tackle. Cutler dove for the pavement.

Rafe hugged his body around Josie's and lifted her off her feet, spinning to take the brunt of the blast as the car exploded and knocked them to the ground. Fire burned through the sleeves of his jacket and seared his right side before they slid to a stop. Josie held on tight and screamed against his neck as bits of hot metal and molten plastic rained down from the smoke-blackened sky above them.

"I DON'T SUPPOSE there's any chance that bomb could be the work of Robbie's loan shark?" Josie ignored the fatigue that made every movement feel like she was dragging her bruised body through deep ocean water, and tossed the gauze she'd been using to treat the scrapes on Rafe's left hand into the trash.

"No."

Rafe took up more than his share of space in the small, curtained-off bay of the Truman Medical Center emergency room. The heat from his body reflected off every polished surface, warming the chilly hospital air. And the coppery scent of blood and antiseptic from his wounds, tinged with the more pungent odors of tar and asphalt imbedded in their clothes from their sliding impact with the pavement filled her head with every breath.

"This was definitely about you." He hooked one finger beneath the sleeve of the green scrubs top she'd changed into when they'd arrived. His eyes lingered on the graze that marred her own elbow until she shrugged away from his touch and rolled the tray of supplies she was using to the other side of the examination table where he sat. "I talked to Sammy and Marco's boss and paid off Robbie's debt on the proviso that they won't do business with Robbie again. And if I hear of them doing business, period, in the Shamrock's neighborhood, I've got a couple of friends in Vice that I'll sic on them."

"I thought you said paying them off would keep Uncle Robbie from learning his lesson."

"I didn't want you to worry about him right now when you should be thinking of yourself. And I needed to narrow down the possibilities of where any threat to you might come from." It seemed she owed a lot more than her life to this man. He stretched his booted feet down to the floor and stood. "Now I wish you'd lie down and let that other nurse who checked you out stitch me up."

"Sit." Josie braced her palm at the center of his chest and pushed him back to his seat on the edge of the table. "I got permission to treat you for a reason. I need to do this. I need to be in control of something in my life. For a few minutes, at least. You're going to be my patient right now, understand?"

"Okay. Whatever you say." Although he let her work without further argument, he perched there like a coiled panther, watching every move she made, no doubt ready to strike should she show any sign of weakness. "But I'm not that bad off. Robbie and Alex got hurt worse."

Josie felt like prey beneath his intense scrutiny, so she focused on her hands and training, and avoided direct contact with those ever-watchful eyes of his. "Robbie was admitted because they had to sedate him to set his leg. Alex was treated for cuts and abrasions and released. Audrey came to pick him up—and my impression is that she won't let him do anything he shouldn't for a few days."

"Yeah, Audrey likes to be in charge."

"She was sick with worry, too. You could see it in her eyes when she first came in with Captain Cutler to check on Alex." Josie risked a glance up into those whiskey-brown eyes and wondered if Rafe had any idea just how frightened *she'd* been to see the shredded sleeve of his jacket and the blood seeping from the wounds he'd sustained saving her. "I hate that other people are getting hurt because of me. I hate the thought of our baby being in danger. Detective Montgomery has to catch the RGK soon. I want to look in his eyes and say that's him, and have him put away where he can't hurt anyone I care about ever again."

"Jose—"

"Stupid hormones." She blinked away the tears stinging her eyes and reached for the scissors on her tray before Rafe could say or do something kind that would undermine whatever fragile sense of power over her own life she had left. "Hope this wasn't a favorite shirt of yours," she apologized before snipping away the tattered remnants of his shirtsleeve.

She gently cradled his wrist and elbow to turn the raw skin of his forearm into the light above the table. She winced at the idea that his arm would have been scraped down to the bone if he hadn't been wearing his thick leather jacket. And even with the snack Captain

Cutler had brought her from the vending machine to eat earlier, her stomach rolled with the knowledge that it could have been her face or back or belly and the baby sleeping inside needing emergency medical treatment if Rafe hadn't put himself between her and the exploding heat and flying metal of the car bomb.

She felt his tender hand brush aside the tendril of hair that had fallen across one eye. "Jose, you're dead on your feet."

"Poor choice of words, Sergeant." She shook her hair back, indicating the wayward strand was beyond his reach.

"You know what I mean…ow!"

"Shh." She was peeling away the rest of his shirt now, gently pulling it off his shoulders to expose his right flank and the cut beneath the dark, moist stain on his shirt. She tossed the remains of the shirt into the trash and eyed the gash where debris from the explosion had sliced through his skin. "This is the wound I'm worried about."

"I've had worse," he hissed through his teeth as she probed the wound with her gloved fingers.

Josie reached for a bottle of saline and a rinse tray, then urged him to cross his arm over his chest and expose the injury for a clearer view. He still wore his gun and badge clipped to his belt, and with a little more twisting and repositioning of the lights, she finally got the view she wanted.

Along with a sight she never would have believed.

"Oh, my God. Rafe." Thin white stripes cut across the tanned skin of his back. They were old scars, dozens of them, faded slash marks crisscrossing from his shoulder blades down beneath the waist of his jeans, as if he'd been whipped. Repeatedly. Josie's vision clouded as she traced the marks of violence across his skin. "Are these from...your dad?"

In passing, he'd mentioned the abuse he'd suffered growing up, had used it as a reason for not wanting a family of his own. But she'd never seen the evidence, not even that night in his truck. Of course, she'd been a little preoccupied that night. Her heart had been wide open, her senses on fire with Rafe's explosive need. Even then, she hadn't fully realized the depth of his understanding about violence toward children.

But, as usual, Rafe wasn't one to talk about details. Even as she became aware of the trail of goose bumps popping up behind her touch on his skin, he was gently pulling her hands away and ducking his head to catch her gaze squarely with his. With the pad of his thumb, he wiped away the tears burning her cheeks. "None of that now. We've got plenty enough to worry about tonight." He silenced any discussion on the matter. "You stitch me up, nurse, and let's get out of here."

"I'm not officially a nurse until graduation."

"You think I want any other woman's hands on me?"

The unexpected timing of his humor surprised a smile out of her. Cupping the side of his jaw to both comfort and thank him, Josie kissed the corner of his mouth, sniffed back her tears and went to work. With a tender efficiency, she cleaned and stitched the wound, gave him a shot of antibiotics after clearing her treatment with the supervisor, and bandaged him up with gauze and tape.

As bossy and taciturn and guarded and demanding

as he could be, Rafe had done nothing but take care of her. As long as she'd known him, he'd been big brother, protector, confidant, friend—he'd opened up his emotions to her more than he ever had with anyone else, and he'd put his life on the line for her, despite his reservations about the baby and a future together. Whether he believed it or not, Rafe Delgado cared about her. Maybe he even loved her as much as a man like him could. He'd been wounded, inside and out, by life, and he'd faced most of those demons—he'd survived them—all by himself. For the time it took to doctor his wounds and give him the care that every human being deserved, Josie would take care of *him*.

"There," she finally announced, peeling off her gloves and tossing them into the secure receptacle with the other bio waste. "You're done."

"I think you might have a future in this line of work," he teased.

"Ha, ha." She rolled the tray back into place and made note of the supplies she'd used on the computer. "Now I recommend rest and light activities for a few days, so you don't rip the stitches out."

"Am I allowed to move now?"

"Of course."

"Then come here." He snagged her wrist and pulled her right between his legs against the table. "This is the only kind of healing I need."

Muffling her startled yelp, he captured her lips in a kiss. His hands settled at either side of her waist, then slid upward to tangle in her hair and tilt her mouth to a more intimate angle so he could plunge his tongue inside and brand her with his textures and taste. The kiss was hard and deep and full of a possessive claim that turned Josie molten inside.

"I thought I'd lost you," he whispered against her mouth.

She braced her hands against his bare chest, tickling her palms with the dusting of crisp, dark hair. Fatigue ebbed out and energy seeped in through the feverish contact with her fingertips.

Rafe loved her. He *had* to love her. How could a man kiss her like this? Care like this? Need like this, and not feel the same way she felt about him?

"When I saw all the blood on you, I was so afraid," she confessed, leaning in, rising on tiptoe, winding her arms around his neck. She needed to feel his whole body pressed against her. Hard planes against soft curves, his abundant warmth infusing her with heat. "I don't want to lose anyone else, Rafe. I can't lose—"

"Get a room."

The swish of the curtain cordoning off this side of the room echoed like thunder in her ears. Rafe went still beneath her touch. He pulled his mouth from her grasping lips and rested his forehead against hers for a moment before nudging her back a step and standing.

"I thought we had one," Rafe answered, keeping one hand at Josie's waist, perhaps sensing the weariness and confusion crashing through her at the abrupt end to the embrace. He turned to catch the black T-shirt Trip Jones tossed at him. "Your timing sucks, big guy."

"Yeah, but I've got a big black van parked outside to escort you to your destination."

Rafe waited for a nod that she could stand on her own two feet before releasing her to slip into the clean shirt. Josie gathered her composure enough to catch the hem as he stretched it over his shoulders and chest, to guide it safely over the wound in his side. The reality was, a killer was out there who wanted her dead. And these men had risked their lives to save her. She wouldn't complain about a lost kiss when they were already sacrificing so much for her.

"And your wife?" Rafe asked, tucking the shirt beneath his badge and gun. "She's not safe with the RGK out there, either."

Trip was holding two Kevlar vests in addition to the one he wore. He handed them both to Rafe, who pulled one on and strapped it beneath his arms before slipping the other over Josie's head.

The weight of the protective vest pulling at her shoulders was a tangible reminder of the burden of knowledge she carried. "Is this necessary?" she asked, helping Rafe adjust the Velcro straps so that the vest stretched far enough to shield the baby, as well.

"Yes," Rafe answered without hesitation.

Trip waited until Josie's vest was secure before gesturing to the exit behind him. "I dropped Charlotte off to stay with her friend, Audrey, Alex Taylor's fiancée. Even beat up like he is, Alex will be armed to the teeth if I know him. So you, Sergeant, are stuck with me."

Randy Murdock poked her head around the corner, "And me."

"What about my truck?" Rafe asked.

"It's going to need some serious body work, but it'll drive," Randy reported. "I'll deliver it as soon as the crime lab releases it. Having it between you and the bulk of that explosion is probably what saved your lives." She adjusted the rifle she carried over her shoulder and patted the SWAT letters on her Kevlar. "That's why the captain ordered vests for everyone until we bring this guy in."

Guns. Vests. Violence. Rafe and his coworkers were talking so matter-of-factly, as if what was happening to her was an everyday event in their lives. When had they talked? How had they planned this? SWAT Team One was moving like a well-oiled machine, and she was the cog who didn't fit in. "Where is the captain?" she asked.

Michael Cutler walked up behind Randy Murdock. "Not to worry. We've got control of the scene and the situation." He winked at Josie, then slipped into a steely posture that Rafe and the others instantly responded to. "Are you ready to move out or are we going to stand around and chat all night? Montgomery's got Lassen tied up in an interview room at HQ, and the rest of the press following the case are at the scene of the explosion, hassling Nick Fensom and the CSIs there. This is our window of opportunity. We have a witness to escort to a safe house. Let's get moving."

Josie, in a bit of a panic, reached for Rafe's hand as he moved out to follow the others toward the E.R. exit. "What safe house? I'm really not in control of any part of my life anymore, am I?"

He squeezed her hand in reassurance. Then he tugged her to his side to press a kiss to her temple and pull her into step with him. His touch gave her the only bit of comfort she could hold on to. "We're going to my place, Jose. We're taking you home."

WHAT THE HELL happened tonight? How could he be so far off his game that no one had died? He paced the sidewalk back and forth, well beyond the eyes and ears of the cops swarming the lot behind the Shamrock Bar. He drew in deep drags on his cigarette, waiting for the nicotine to kick in, but found no relief for the anger coursing through his blood.

He'd even had his camera all set up to record the perfect memento of his handiwork. He tossed the useless device through the open window of his vehicle, gritting his teeth when it smacked against the tripod he'd stowed earlier. He rolled the cigarette between his thumb and forefinger, squeezing it between his lips as he breathed in, filling up his lungs with pungent smoke and rage.

They'd cleared the bar as he'd expected, the chaos of emptying a busy establishment on a Saturday night giving him plenty of opportunity to move the car into place near the cop's truck—close enough to do the damage he wanted, but not close enough to raise suspicion until it was too late. The bomb had detonated perfectly. And not one of those hero wannabes had even suspected anything was amiss with the bar owner's car.

But there'd been too many people there tonight. People he hadn't counted on. People who didn't belong in the middle of one of his plans. He should have planned for every contingency, every variable beyond the woman, her drunk uncle and the overzealous boyfriend. He was smarter than that. Smarter than her. Smarter than all of them.

With the need to do violence creeping out of every pore, he flung the cigarette to the ground. But the shower of sparks floating up from the concrete reminded him of the lesson he'd learned from the time he could put the letters together—never leave any DNA behind.

With a muffled curse, he picked up the glowing butt and ground it out in his palm. The pain was intense, but brief. He'd endured worse growing up, at the hands of his father and uncles. He had the polka-dot scars behind his right shoulder from the time they'd first taught him that smoking was a bad habit—not because the chemicals could kill him, but because his saliva could leave something for the cops to trace behind him.

One of the flyers that had been handed out earlier to the crowd of patrons and reporters who were curious about the Shamrock Bar's emergency shut down blew across his path. He stomped on it with his foot and then lifted it toward the light of the street lamp on the corner. There was his picture, looking back at him, although it barely qualified as a likeness. He'd learned enough about altering his appearance and manner to blend in anywhere.

But Josie Nichols could bring him into focus. If she ever got close enough, ever looked him straight in the eye…she'd know he was the man she'd bumped into the day he'd eliminated Kyle Austin. He couldn't allow her to see him, to stop him before he'd completed his work.

Crumpling the KCPD flyer in his fist, he stuffed it into his pocket along with the dead cigarette. Then he held his palm up to the same light and licked the raw mark of the cigarette burn there. The momentary pain was enough to distract him, to clear the blinding anger from his thoughts and pull him back to the moment at hand.

No woman was going to outsmart him. He wanted Josie Nichols dead. And so she would be.

He'd watched her, photographed her, talked to her. He'd looked her in the eyes when she'd been an insignificant speck in his life and he'd looked at her again when she could bring his work to an abrupt end—before everyone he needed to kill was dead—before he would finally know satisfaction, justice and rest.

Inhaling a breath of the cool night air, he gathered his wits about him and turned his back to the swirling red and blue lights, and yellow crime-scene tape. He climbed inside his vehicle and immediately straightened up the mess he'd left there. The tripod needed to lie flat on the floor behind the seat. The camera needed to be returned to the proper compartment of its carrying case. He pulled the fabric refresher from the glove compartment and sprayed his clothes, needing to get rid of the lingering smell of smoke that clung to him.

And then he saw the bright green neon of the Shamrock Bar's front window sign and smiled at the fortunate omen. There were three leaves on a shamrock. Three. The tension inside him evaporated and everything came into balance.

Two members of KCPD's SWAT Team One had thwarted his efforts to destroy his intended victims, but the third one with the temper would not.

His first attempt to abduct Josie Nichols from the hospital and kill her in a more private location had failed.

Ditto with the bomb. His second attempt at murder had failed.

But the third time would be the charm.

Josie would be his third female victim in Kansas City. This would be his third attempt.

Three was perfection.

He laughed out loud as he started the engine. He checked his side view mirror once, twice, three times before pulling out into the deserted street. This time, he'd put his considerable skills to the test. He'd do Josie Nichols right under the noses of KCPD and SWAT Team One.

And then he'd be free again.

Chapter Ten

Josie tossed in her sleep, desperately trying to wake herself. But the terrors in her dreams refused to let her go.

"Help me. Help me!" she cried, her voice lost in the rush of wind whistling past her ears. She was flying through the air, propelled by clouds of fire. Flaming tendrils reached out like clawing hands, grabbing at her limbs, singeing her skin.

And then she was falling, crashing down into the darkness. Black shadows swirled around her, blinded her eyes, swallowed her up in a bone-deep chill. "Stop." She was losing her strength now. The ping-pong effect of heat and chill, light and dark, flying and falling, was confusing her mind, draining her energy, exhausting her spirit. "Stop it. Please."

The chill remained as the darkness turned and took form. She was surrounded by so many shadows. They reached out, tangled in her hair, touched her face. She jerked away, but there was another shadow, curling around her arm, pulling her farther into the abyss. "No. Stop!"

She tore herself free, but there were other shadows, other hands, waiting. She was buffeted from unwanted touch to unwanted touch. They had her feet, her hands.

They were pulling her down, pinning her helplessly in the dark, descending upon her.

"Help..." One stuffed up her mouth. Another touched her belly. No!

She couldn't move. She had no control. The shadows played with her at will. No matter how she twisted, how she fought, she couldn't escape.

More hands were on her now—shapeless, darkly translucent hands—but with strength, with purpose, with a terrible intent as they pressed down on her belly and seeped beneath her skin to find the precious life she carried inside. And every place they touched was cold, so cold. She was too cold to move, too cold to fight. They were killing her. Killing her baby. Killing.

Josie screamed and thrashed valiantly against the unseen faces in the shadows. But there were so many and she was so alone.

"Help me. Help," she begged.

Some of the shadows parted, giving her a glimpse of light. Not the burning fire of before, but a cold, dark light. The faces took form. Some were distorted, some masked. But the eyes on every face were the same—icy, colorless, evil. "No."

The eyes moved nearer as cold shadow fingers closed around her throat. Josie clawed at the hands choking her, but they were all mist and malevolence. Strength, but no substance. She had nothing to fight. They were squeezing the very life out of her and her unborn child, and she was powerless to stop them.

Other faces took shape in the mist. Her father. Patrick. Uncle Robbie. She reached out for help, begged

*them not to leave her—to save her, protect her, love her.
But one by one, they turned away, leaving her alone in
the shadows.*

"No. Don't leave me. Don't leave me!"

*The eyes vanished and the shadows swirled around
her, filling her inside and out with their darkness.*

"Josie." The hands were on her shoulders, shaking
her, keeping her from reaching out.

"No. Don't leave..." She slapped at the hands,
twisted free.

"Wake up." These hands were warm. They had substance. "Honey, come on, you're scaring me."

Josie went still. She slowly blinked and peered
through her lashes. There was light. The shadows were
gone. Her hands flew to her belly and throat. She was
safe. They were safe.

She opened her eyes fully and saw warm, whiskey-
brown eyes, hovering above her, full of concern. The
hands on her were real. The eyes were real.

And she was safe.

"Rafe?"

He sat on the edge of the bed, his broad shoulders
heaving with a deep breath as he released her. "That
was quite a nightmare."

"Rafe!" Fully awake now, Josie scrambled to sit up.
With Rafe's help, she kicked and tugged to free her legs
from the sheet and blanket. And then she was on her
knees, flinging her arms around his neck and holding
tight to the one tangible constant in her life. "Don't
leave me, Rafe. Everybody leaves."

He wound his arms around her, plastering her to his
bare chest, letting her feel his heat and hardness and

the solid reality of his presence. He rubbed his stubbly cheek against hers. "I won't, honey. I won't leave you. You're not alone."

RAFE SQUINTED HIS eye open at the pesky beam of afternoon sunlight filtering through the blinds at the living room window.

He was probably going to wind up with a permanent crick in his neck from so many nights sleeping on a couch that was too short for his long frame. But somehow, today, he didn't seem to mind the discomfort—not when he had a mile of creamy long legs tangled with his, and the citrusy scent of Josie's long hair spilled across his arms and chest as he spooned behind her on the couch.

When her scream had wakened him at eight this morning, he'd gone flying into the bedroom with nothing more than his Glock and his pajama pants. His fear that Donny Kemp had somehow gotten past him and the SWAT cop parked outside his building had morphed into an equally disturbing, but very different type of fear when he found Josie thrashing under the covers. Tears wet her cheeks as she slept, and her plaintive cries reached deep beneath his emotional armor and ripped his heart in two.

He hadn't known what to do except set his gun out of the way on the bedside table and wake her. She'd been clinging to him ever since. And he hadn't let go.

He'd cradled Josie in his lap and rocked her back and forth until the tears had stopped. The wound in his side throbbed and his bruised and battered arms ached the longer he sat with her, but he refused to move. He'd held her like that for an endless time, with nothing but one of his black KCPD T-shirts that she'd borrowed for a night-shirt between them. Once she was cried out, and had shared the horrors of her dreams—a nightmare about feeling helpless and abandoned and completely at the mercy of the RGK that made his blood simmer—she'd dozed off, her soft cheek nestled against his shoulder.

Rafe had considered tucking her back into bed. But he didn't want to be a room away from her anymore, and the intimacy of sharing a bed—of sharing *his* bed—spoke of commitment and answering to dead fathers and wanting a thing so badly he couldn't think straight. He wanted Josie. He wanted those beautiful smiles. He wanted those soft lips reaching for his. He wanted the warmth of her curvy body and compassionate spirit to wrap him up and make him feel needed, wanted, whole. The idea of lying in his bed with Josie, even with covers demurely tucked between them, aroused something primal inside Rafe. It made him think she could truly be his, that he could open up his heart and believe his feelings would be safe with her.

But guilt and killers and a lesson learned early in life reminded him that he didn't deserve the precious woman—the precious family—he held in his arms.

So he wound up carrying her out here to the sofa to watch over her while she caught up on her much-needed sleep. He'd fed her a snack and waited for her to use the restroom around lunchtime, but then she'd come back to him because she was afraid the nightmare would return. They'd sat together and he did a lot of listening while she chatted about this and that—good memories of her father, Robbie's broken leg and who would run the bar in his absence, the crib that Rafe insisted he buy to replace the junker in her apartment.

She was leaning against his shoulder, nodding off again before he could answer where he'd gotten the money to pay off Robbie's loan shark. It was just as well. Mentioning the one thing of value his parents had left him—a small inheritance—would have spoiled the mood. He was liking this calm, this quiet he shared with Josie. Being with her seemed to soothe any anger, resentment or fear buried inside him. Being with Josie filled up a well of emptiness that he was only aware of when she was around, because it reminded him of how little he had that mattered when she wasn't.

When she'd shivered with the chill of the apartment's air-conditioning, he'd curled up beside her to give her the heat of his body. Finally, knowing his friends were keeping a round-the-clock watch on his apartment, fatigue claimed him, too.

Now he was wide awake and his body was on fire. Her sweet little derriere was nestled right against him and he was shamelessly aroused. A breast that was fuller, firmer than he remembered strained against the cup of his hand through the thin cotton barrier separating them. His other hand rested with a possessive claim on her hip.

What excuse could he make now about keeping his distance? He'd made a tactical error in thinking his bed was the only place where this raw intimacy could get inside his head and make him think this was how good his life could be.

Rafe nuzzled his lips against the crown of her hair, willing his body to cool its desire before his baser urges broke the spell of serenity surrounding them. He tried to imagine what Aaron would say to him. Maybe nothing so crass as *"Get your hands off my daughter,"* but definitely something that would make him think before he acted. *"Are you sure that's what you want? Remember your promise to protect her. I don't want my little girl to get hurt. So be sure—be very sure you're the man who'll always cherish her."*

His fingers slid, ever so lightly, around the curve of Josie's hip. He could feel the taut stretch of her skin through the plain cotton panties she wore. Would he feel the same way if this was *his* daughter? Would he give the same sort of speech to a son when it came time to discuss the facts of life? Would he be around when that time came? Would he be any part of Josie's life then?

Holding the rest of his body perfectly still so as not to wake her, he brushed his fingers along the hem of the T-shirt she wore, silently measuring the growing curve of her belly. What would Aaron say about how Rafe had treated his daughter now? Would the excitement of having a grandchild override any blame he might place?

And then he felt the tremor in Josie's tummy and he snatched his hand away. Was that a muscle spasm? Had he disturbed the baby's slumber?

With curiosity drawing him as much as trepidation was warning him away, Rafe lifted his arm and moved his hand around Josie again. He'd read in his book that the mother could feel the baby's movements even before the sixth month of her pregnancy. Could he? His hand hovered over her belly. His fingertips brushed the T-shirt she wore.

"Here." Josie splayed her fingers over his hand and pulled it firmly against her.

Too late. He realized from the changing rhythm of her breathing that Josie was awake. "Sorry, I didn't mean to wake…"

Rafe fell silent as she guided his hand to the ripples of movement inside her.

"You have every right to get to know Junior, too," she whispered, shifting from her side onto her back.

Her sweet, round bottom rubbed against him, stirring things to life again. But Rafe was too awestruck by the baby's movements to immediately notice Josie's effect on him.

The baby rolled inside her, almost pushing against his hand as if eager to meet Daddy's touch. Rafe raised himself up on one elbow to see if he could see what he was feeling. Josie pulled up the hem of her T-shirt to let him see the subtle shifts in her belly. Amazing.

"I told you the little one likes to be active when I'm trying to rest."

"Is it…?" That was wrong. Rafe corrected himself the way Josie once had. This was a real, living child moving beneath his hand. *His* child. "Is the baby okay? After that tumble across the parking lot last night? Are you hurting any?"

Still holding his palm on her belly, Josie reached up with her other hand to stroke her fingers across his jaw. "Other than a few scrapes, the doctor at Truman cleared me. I'll call my OB later just to make sure. But Junior's fine. I'm fine. Thanks to you."

When she slid her hand behind his neck to bring his mouth down to hers, Rafe didn't hesitate. He returned the chaste kiss Josie offered. When he pulled away, her eyes were looking straight up into his. Pools of deep blue beauty, they sent him a dozen messages. "Sometimes you make me crazy, Delgado. And sometimes you make me want to cry." A tear sparkled in the clear blue depths, but she blinked it away. "You've never touched a pregnant belly, have you?"

He shook his head and turned his gaze to see the wonder of how perfectly his hand spanned the bump where the baby was playing another round of pinball. He hated the memory that crept into his head. "I remember my parents getting into a fight once. My mother wanted to have another baby, I guess." The vile words constricted his chest. "He told her he wasn't going to live with a fat cow he couldn't have sex with the way it had been when she was pregnant with me."

"Oh, my God. Rafe." Josie pushed herself up to a sitting position, momentarily breaking the contact between them.

But Rafe didn't want any space between them. He scooped her up and sat her on his lap. There was no hiding his desire pulsing against her thigh. He brushed the fall of hair out of her eyes so she could read the sincerity in his. "You're beautiful, Jose." With a little less hesitation this time, he cupped his hand over her belly. Her hand was there immediately to link them together. He shook his head. "I can't imagine any man thinking like that, saying such an ugly thing. The baby only enhances your curves. Your skin is so soft and pink. There's nothing more feminine and womanly..." His fingers were tunneling into the rich silk of her hair. "I've always thought you were so beautiful. But now..."

She tiptoed her fingers around his neck. "Now…?"

Something earthy and hungry lit a fuse that burned through his blood. "The book I'm reading says you can safely make love well into your third trimester—as long as it's comfortable for you and you're having a healthy pregnancy."

Josie's fingers tightened at his nape. "I'm very healthy."

Rafe turned her in his lap, splaying her legs open to straddle him. "I want you, Josie. I want to show you how beautiful I think you are. I want to do this right and be the man that you deserve."

She pressed her fingers over his lips, silencing him. "The man I deserve? You saved my life, rescued me from my nightmares and just shared a priceless, tender moment when you felt the baby for the first time. How could you ever doubt…?" He could see the temper brewing in her eyes, but he could see something else there, too. "Like I said, words aren't your best thing. Maybe you'd better show me what you're feeling."

She rose up onto her knees to replace her fingers with her lips. The sweet innocence of her kiss lasted for only a few seconds. Then her fingers were digging into his shoulders. Her breasts were pillowing against his chest. And when she moaned with the same frustration building inside him, her lips parted and he deepened the kiss, letting her explore his mouth with the same brazen thoroughness with which he plundered hers.

In a flurry of greedy tongues and stroking hands that was every bit as needy as that first time they'd made love, Rafe stripped the shirt off her and closed his mouth over the hard tip of her taut, responsive breast.

He licked, he squeezed, he pulled on her until her hands were fisting in his hair, locking his mouth against her as she whispered, "More. More."

She writhed in his lap, peppered kisses over his eyes and jaw, nipped at the unexpected bundle of nerves cording along the side of his neck. Despite the rapid countdown of the time bomb ticking inside him, Rafe was determined to make this last, to make this right for Josie.

Capturing her close to his chest, he stood, anchoring his hands beneath her bottom and urging her to wrap her legs around him and hold on while he carried her into the bedroom and laid her on top of the tangled covers. Rafe quickly shed his pants and followed her down, shifting onto his side to avoid putting any pressure on her belly.

"Beautiful." He kissed her temple, nuzzled her neck, swept his tongue over the distended peak of her breast. "So beautiful."

"Rafe." His name was a husky gasp that teased his ears and settled like a caress deep inside him. "Rafe."

He hooked a finger beneath the elastic of her panties and tugged them down her legs, inch by inch, kissing each new curve, each new hollow, each irresistible expanse of velvety skin until she was sitting up, sliding her hands over his hot skin, begging him to end the sweet torment.

Rafe eased her back onto the pillows and crawled over her, holding himself up on his hands and knees as he leaned down to reclaim her lips. His arousal brushed against her belly, nudged against her thighs. Her breasts rose and fell with deep, ragged breaths that matched his own. And as she welcomed him into her mouth, mating her tongue to his, she flattened her palms against his chest, scraped her fingers over his taut nipples and sent a shock wave of desire straight down to his straining shaft. Then, as if sensing her own power over him, she reached down and took him in her hand.

Lurching into her soft grip, he tore his mouth from hers and sucked in a deep breath. "Easy, honey. I'm trying to go slow."

Her eyes were wicked with their lack of sympathy for his plight, her pupils dilated with passion. "I don't need slow. I need you."

The wound on his side was beginning to ache with his effort to rein in everything he was feeling, to hold himself back until she was ready, until he was certain. "I don't want to hurt you." He lifted a handful of her sable-dark hair where it fanned against the pillow and buried his nose in its delectable softness. "I don't want it to be like the last time."

Josie released him to frame his face with that sure, gentle touch of hers. "Remember how I said that, sometimes, one partner needs more than the other?"

He nodded. "I needed you that night."

Her answering smile made the message clear. "I need you now."

And then there were no more words.

Rafe slipped his fingers inside her, tested her readiness, had her twisting and slick and begging for completion. He bent her legs and slipped her feet onto his shoulders, taking great care not to put any pressure on her belly as he slid inside her. He stroked her with his thumb as he filled her up and she flew apart, curling her fists into the sheets and crying out her pleasure. Her body convulsed around him and he was no longer able to deny his own release. With one final push into her welcoming heat, the fuse inside him detonated.

The aftershocks soon abated, taking the last bit of tension with them and leaving Rafe feeling as weary and sated as the sweet smile he kissed on Josie's lips.

Aaron Nichols could have his hide. Tomorrow. This afternoon Rafe was lying down beside Josie, pulling the blanket over their cooling bodies. She turned onto her side and he curled up behind her, skin to skin, his hand possessively cupping the swell of her abdomen where her baby slept—where *their* baby slept. For a few more minutes of peaceful slumber, this was his woman. This was his family.

And Rafael Delgado let himself love and be loved in return.

PERFECT.

He put the plastic cap on the end of the tiny vial and slid it between the prongs of his ring. He practiced the delivery system one time—a simple handshake, a friendly grasp on the shoulder, an accidental touch while helping someone who'd tripped over her own feet. Press firmly and voilá, poison delivered. Toxin rushes through bloodstream, throat swells, target dead.

Not even a fast-thinking nurse with trauma training could save the victim's life in time.

He could deliver the drug and be on the other side of the park, well beyond suspicion before anyone in Josie Nichols's well-armed entourage even guessed what had happened.

No one was in his head calling him *stupid* now. This time, he'd planned for every contingency. There were backups to his backup plan. This time he would not let the woman beat him.

He put away the chemicals and returned to the mirror over his dresser where he adjusted his tie. The jacket was a necessary cover if he wanted to blend in at the KCPD carnival.

Then he opened the top drawer of his dresser—once, twice, three times before pulling out the Beretta pistol. He checked the magazine to see that it was still clean and loaded, and then tucked it beneath his jacket into the holster strapped to his belt. The small brick of C-4 with its hodgepodge of timers and wires would serve its purpose, too.

He knew any number of ways to kill, and had used most of them. He'd have whatever method he needed on hand when he left for work this morning.

Josie Nichols would be dead by the end of the day.

Chapter Eleven

"Okay, people, are we ready to go to work?" After clapping his hands to get their attention, Jeffrey Beecher adjusted his glasses on his nose and waited for everyone inside the blue-and-white-striped carnival tent to stop fussing with their uniforms and find a seat for their final instructions.

Josie pulled a handkerchief from the pocket of her black apron and dabbed at the perspiration dotting her forehead. Although the weather was unseasonably warm for the Memorial Day weekend, there was no sign of rain in the forecast. Clarice Darnell and Mr. Beecher had decided to go ahead and make the KCPD Carnival fundraiser an outdoor event. Although why her temporary boss would wear a suit and tie to an event that was one part picnic, one part circus sideshow and one part street fair was beyond her.

Not even the cops who were in attendance were wearing their uniforms—with five notable exceptions.

Rafe paced a line in the grass beside her chair. The rolled-up sleeves of his black SWAT uniform were the only concession to the heat. "This is the most irresponsible idea I've ever heard," he muttered as she took her seat in one of the folding chairs set up between the ice machines, soda-filled coolers and catering supplies set up inside the tent.

Josie tugged at the collar of her white blouse. "Smile, and pretend you're having fun."

Rafe glared down at her.

"Okay, then, at least try not to scare anybody."

He didn't laugh. There hadn't been much laughter between them lately, not since last Sunday afternoon when they'd made love, when she'd nearly wept at the tenderness Rafe showed with the baby. As desperately as he wanted to be a part of a family, he was equally wary of doing just that. It was a frightening thing, giving one's love and trust over to another person. What if that person died? Went to prison? Didn't love you back? She understood Rafe's need to belong to someone far better than he gave her credit for. Over the past few months she'd learned that a man could be closer to her making eye contact across a crowded bar than he was holding her as she slept each night. Perhaps they'd gone too far. They'd revealed too much of what was deepest in their hearts, and Rafe had retreated back inside his solitary armor.

There hadn't been any laughter at all since she'd met with Spencer Montgomery for an update on her case, and she'd agreed with his request to maintain as normal a life as possible, under the continued watch of SWAT Team One, of course. His suggestion had made sense—that locking herself away in a safe house would only drive the RGK underground. But if she continued her nurse's training, continued to work, then Donny Kemp might drop his guard and make a mistake. If there was some chance that he could get to her, then he'd be more likely to show himself. And though the thought of coming face-to-face with him again terrified her, the sooner she could spot him—the sooner KCPD could arrest him—then the sooner she'd have the chance to prepare for her baby's arrival, and to, quite possibly, prepare herself for a life without Rafe.

So, instead of laughing, he eyed the rear flap of the tent where Trip Jones was standing guard, the front entrance manned by Michael Cutler and Alex Taylor, and then pressed a button on the radio clipped to the epaulet at his shoulder. "Murdock. This is Sarge. What's the status out there?"

An answering buzz of static garnered the attention of the other servers and event staff sitting around her. But Rafe's sharp gaze turned them away just as quickly.

Josie knew that Miranda Murdock was stationed somewhere outside, on high ground, as Rafe had put it. With a pair of high-powered binoculars and a clear view of most of the park and the crowds gathering there, Randy was there to alert them to any trouble before it could reach Josie. "It's all normal out here," Randy reported. "The crowd's picking up, as expected, but most of them probably won't head to the food tents until closer to lunchtime. I don't see anyone matching the description Detective Montgomery issued. I don't see anyone behaving in a suspicious manner, either."

"Keep me posted."

"Will do. Murdock out."

Josie looked up at him before the pacing resumed. "Satisfied?"

"Hardly. Do you think I want to lose you two to this guy?"

You *two?*

Maybe he hadn't resurrected that armor as securely as she'd thought.

She reached for his hand to stop him as he walked past. "Rafe."

He squeezed her hand, but pulled away. "Not now, Jose. I need to be thinking like a cop."

Jeffrey Beecher clapped his hands and silenced them again. "Most of you will be responsible for clearing the picnic tables and keeping the chafing dishes on the serving tables full." Josie and a handful of others had been charged with carrying pitchers of water, iced tea and lemonade, and providing refills for the patrons to keep traffic flow amongst the tables to a minimum. "Ms. Darnell will handle ticket sales and donations, and I'll be overseeing the service at lunch and dinner. Remember, we want our guests and patrons to enjoy their fried chicken and funnel cakes. But we also want to feed them and move them along so we can make room for new customers." His businesslike manner became effusive as he rallied the staff. "We're here to raise money for a good cause today." His gaze seemed to touch every employee, including Josie. "So when your feet get tired, or the trays get too heavy, just remember the children and families we're doing this for."

There were a few cheers and a mild round of applause.

Apparently, that wasn't the reaction he'd wanted. He put up his hand to motion the few who'd begun to move back to their seats. "Think of the single moms and the orphans—and let's make some money."

The audience's more robust reaction seemed to

satisfy him. After checking in with Clarice Darnell over the earbud he wore, he clapped his hands for the third time and dismissed them. "The food tents are officially open for business. Let's get to work."

Captain Cutler radioed that he'd spotted Spencer Montgomery and was going over to meet with him. Alex and Trip kept a close eye on the other food workers going in and out of the tent. With her lanky, moody shadow following at a distance behind her, Josie went to work loading plastic pitchers with ice and setting them on a tray to fill with drinks.

"Miss Nichols?"

She was up to her wrists in ice when Jeffrey Beecher summoned her. Leaving the scoop in the machine, she dried her hands on her apron and turned to face him. "Yes?"

She jerked back when his hands reached for her throat.

"Easy." He held up his manicured hands, one of which sported a bandage, in apology before reaching toward her again. Backed against the ice machine with no place to run, she followed his fingers in all the way to her collar. He grinned at her sigh of relief and straightened the crisp fold of oxford cloth. "I want you to look your best since you're representing my company."

"Yes, sir."

Before she could look beyond the hands that had invaded her personal space and return his smile, he'd moved on to the next fine-tuning of a uniform and to tell another server to put six pitchers on her tray instead of five.

"I thought this was Ms. Darnell's company."

She'd identified the slightly lispy sneer of her co-worker even before he walked up beside her. "Hi, Bud."

"He's got airs, don't he?"

The lisp came from the toothpick he kept toying at with his tongue. The shiver running down her spine came from the hint of recognition hiding in the corners of her mind. Was it a smell? The faintest trace of cigarette smoke on someone's clothes? Had she seen something familiar without realizing it? Would a few moments alone give her a chance to clear her head and make sense of an impression that might only be wishful thinking?

She bent her knees and lifted the tray of pitchers.

Bud stopped her from swinging the tray up onto her shoulder and tried to pull it from her grasp. "Can I give you a hand with that?"

"No, thanks." She pulled away and lifted again.

"It's got to be heavy."

In an instant Rafe was there, his hand firmly planted beneath Bud Preston's name on his uniform jacket, pushing him back a step. "She said no. Now get to work, Preston. Somewhere else."

The radio on Rafe's uniform buzzed and Michael Cutler's voice commanded his attention. "Sarge—you got a minute? Detective Montgomery's here. Let's go over our coverage assignments for the day, and get him and his partner up to speed on our protection detail so they can fill in, in case we get a call. Can you meet me out front?"

Rafe pressed a button. "Roger that." He glanced over to make sure that Trip was still standing watch at the back of the tent. Then he reached for the collar that Jeffrey Beecher had just straightened and brushed aside a strand of hair that had worked loose from the thick bun at her nape. "I'll be back in a few minutes. You don't leave this tent until I get back unless Trip or Alex is with you. Understand?"

"Roger that."

That almost earned her a smile. But the glimpse of the Rafe who loved and laughed never fully materialized. With a sad, heated look, he strode out of the tent, leaving Josie to shoulder the tray and decode her troublesome thoughts all by herself.

"WE HAVE A BOMB." Alex Taylor's voice came over the radio in sharp, concise tones. An alert like this usually chilled Rafe down to the bone and cleared his head, allowing him to concentrate on the details he needed to hear and let his training kick in. "I repeat, one of the detection dogs has located explosives pinned underneath a car in the parking lot."

There were enough off-duty cops with their families sitting at the tables near where Rafe was standing to overhear the warning and start a general buzz of concern through the crowd. A second call from Captain Cutler silenced them. "SWAT One meet on my twenty. Initiate a general evac. Recruit anyone you know to get this crowd moving in an orderly fashion away from the parking lot."

Trip piped in. "Captain, there are a half dozen picnic shelters on the far side of Willow Lake. Easy walking distance, but secure enough. I suggest we have the crowd reconvene there."

"Agreed."

Several of the people around Rafe nodded, understanding the order and the need for prompt cooperation. But Rafe's gaze centered on Josie, stopped in the
middle of all the picnic tables, holding a pitcher of water
in each hand. There were so many people here, leaving their lunches, gathering their spouses and children
and grandchildren, moving halfway across the park—
leaving Josie standing alone in the middle of a sea of
gingham-checked tablecloths.

Rafe was already moving toward her. "This is
wrong."

Those big blue eyes were frightened. Her knuckles
were white around the pitcher handles. She'd nearly
lost her uncle to a bomb. She could have lost the baby.
She could have been lost herself.

So, of course, her concern was for everyone else. "I
put them all in danger."

"No." He pried the pitchers from her hands and set
them on the nearest table, then wrapped his arm behind
her waist to walk her toward the departing crowd. "This
feels wrong. This many people? The middle of the day?
That's not how our guy works."

"You're scaring me."

"Join the club." Rafe lengthened his stride and moved
her steps into double time to keep up with him. He
turned his mouth to his radio, scanning the crowd,
checking the trees beyond. "Captain. He's here. The
bomb's a diversion. I'm getting Josie out of here."

"Negative. Hand her over to Montgomery."

Rafe had never disobeyed an order from his commanding officer. But he'd be damned if he'd trust Josie

and the baby to anyone who didn't eat and breathe SWAT. "Captain," he pleaded. "Michael. The protection of the crowd of cops is booking it out of here. I need to ensure she's safe."

But Michael Cutler was in charge for a reason. "Sergeant, you're my bomb man. I need your expertise here."

Rafe stopped in his tracks, pulling Josie into the shelter of his body and turning to search out the light tower that rose above the stage at the center of the park. There. He saw the two glints of light reflecting off the lenses of Randy's binoculars. "Murdock. You got eyes on Josie?"

"Yes, Sarge."

He dipped his head to kiss Josie, hard and fast, before pulling away and jogging in the opposite direction from the crowd. "Don't let her out of your sight."

Rafe peeled off his helmet and walked away from the distant flashes and shouted questions from the press corps who had gathered as close to the parking lot as the cordon tape allowed.

"It's a dud." He slipped his arm out of his bomb shield and leaned it up against the back of the SWAT van to report to Captain Cutler. He handed over the brick of plastique explosive to Alex, who boxed it up and stowed it inside the van. "The C-4's real enough. But the wires weren't attached to anything. There's no firing device."

The cadre of reporters shifted to follow him to the van. They'd come to the park this morning to cover a human-interest event, to give the police department and its charity some free PR.

Now they wanted his name. They wanted to know where someone could get C-4 and what a firing device was. They wanted to know if this bomb was a terrorist threat aimed at the Kansas City Police Department—or the city itself.

Rafe wanted one thing. "Sir?"

"Go." Cutler dismissed him and turned to tackle public relations with a curious and frightened press.

Rafe spared one moment to scan the mob of reporters to see if Steve Lassen would dare to show his face. Montgomery hadn't been able to do more than fine him for getting too close to Josie. But he didn't see the arrow-like points of his receding hairline. He didn't hear his obnoxious voice, blaming KCPD and SWAT Team One for ruining his career. But that didn't mean he wasn't here lurking somewhere, maybe even heading to the picnic area to steal another unwanted photo of Josie.

Breaking into a jog, Rafe headed toward the blue-and-white-striped food tent. He buzzed his radio. "Murdock." He gave her a couple of seconds and buzzed again. "Murdock. This is Sarge. Pick up. Murdock!"

Dead air.

Maybe the only thing worse than not hearing one of his teammates answer his call was not hearing the teammate protecting the woman he loved answer him.

"Well, aren't you the dedicated little worker."

Josie's stomach plummeted to her toes at the falsely sweet voice. She dropped the pitcher she'd been rinsing

out and immediately put her hands over her belly.
Where was Rafe? Where was Randy Murdock? Where
was anyone who could protect her?

She was alone. In the tent where Rafe had told her to
stay put, where Randy and the rest of SWAT Team One
was supposedly keeping an eye on her. In the middle of
the biggest day of KCPD's year, with more cops than
could fill Robbie's bar just a short walk away, she was
all alone.

Thank God she had a table and a tub of sudsy water
between them. But not for long. She could hear his
footsteps softly squishing the grass. She could smell the
fresh pungency of a recently smoked cigarette wafting
from his clothes. The enormity of what was about to
transpire made her knees shake. But Junior seemed to
sense her distress and pitched a fit, waking and rolling,
reminding Josie of every loving moment she'd shared
with her baby's father. Junior demanded that she fight.

"You're the RGK." She slowly turned as her nemesis
approached. The first thing she noticed were the miss-
ing glasses. Then she saw him pick up a fresh towel
to wipe his already clean hands. "I saw you kill Kyle
Austin." She looked straight into eyes that were colorless, cold, without conscience. "Mr. Beecher."

He smiled, a gesture she found even more frightening than a spoken threat, and she backed away. He
turned a ring on his finger and wove around one row
of folding chairs, then another, until there was only the
table between them. "Your description doesn't look
anything like me, Miss Nichols."

"I got the eyes right." She glanced toward the ice
machine, tried to gauge how long it would take her to

get past it and out the tent's front flap. "You should know there are SWAT cops here to protect me. I believe several of them have a personal beef with you."

He laughed. But it was an ugly, chilling sound. "Officer Taylor's fiancée destroyed my college career. My father beat me when he learned I'd lost that scholarship and intern program to a woman. No Ivy League for me. No money for my family. And all Officer Jones's wife had to do was say yes, and go to the prom with me."

"So she could be kidnapped." Josie inched her way toward the end of the table. "I know the story. Your family abducted her, tortured her, demanded ransom."

"And my father beat me unconscious because I failed to live up to my part of the scam."

A drop of crystalline moisture glistened off the prong of his ring. There wasn't a stone set there at all, but something clear, something wet. Was that the poison he'd used to murder Kyle Austin? A simple shaking of hands, a prick of the skin, a subtle but deadly injection—explained the blood he'd been wiping from his fingers that day.

Josie cradled her stomach and circled the end of the table. "I'm sorry you were abused, Jeffrey. I pity you and the suffering you must have endured."

"I don't want your pity. I'm not the same boy I was then. I'm not Donny Kemp anymore."

"I pity you because you couldn't rise above your childhood." She thought of one man, tall and strong and oh, so brave. "Being abused isn't an excuse for murdering people."

"Most serial killers were abused as children."

"And some good cops were, too."

He unbuttoned the front of his jacket, revealing the Glock 9 mm he'd tucked into the front of his belt. "Your blonde friend who's supposed to be watching over you out there?" He patted the gun. "She won't be coming to save you." Randy? Josie glanced over her shoulder. She hadn't heard a gunshot. "I did mention I have a little issue with women having power over me, didn't I?"

Josie's pulse hammered in her ears. "What did you do to Randy?"

He held up his hands, his clean, pristine hands. The Rich Girl Killer strangled his victims.

"Randy!" she shouted over her shoulder. "Rafe!"

The shadow from her nightmares was closing in on her.

"What did you do with her rifle? You don't have that stuffed inside your pants." Her back was up against the ice machine now. Her fingers teased the edge of the metal door covering the ice compartment. "They'll find you. They'll hunt you down. I'm not the only one who's seen your face."

"Brava." He held out his hand. Expecting her to take it? To surrender to the inevitable? "Such spirit from someone who has no idea how insignificant she is in this world. Allow me to remind you of your proper place."

Josie slipped around to the front of the machine. She pushed open the door with her hip, then shivered at the blast of cold air from inside.

He crept closer. The maniac who'd killed countless men and women, terrorized her, threatened her life, threatened her baby—threatened her best chance at love and happiness—had the nerve to reach out to touch her hand. With the ring.

The ring!

Josie jerked her hand back before deadly poison could pierce her skin. He stumbled forward at the sudden motion and Josie slammed the door down hard on his hand. "Get away from me!"

Beecher gave a guttural yell, like a wild animal caught in a trap. She didn't wait to see if he was truly injured. She wouldn't turn to see the murderous intent in his eyes. She ran. She shoved chairs behind her to block his path, but she was off balance with the baby, slower than she used to be.

And he was so angry. So terribly, terribly angry.

Her heart pounded wildly in her chest. The baby shifted. *No, sweetie. Not now!*

He grabbed the knot of her hair and jerked her back off her feet. Josie tumbled into his chest, knocking them both to the ground. He landed with a thud, but he was only winded, not down.

Josie rolled, clutching her belly, protecting her baby as chairs toppled and crashed down around her. She got up to her hands and knees and crawled away. But he was faster, stronger. He caught her ankle and gave a vicious jerk, knocking her onto her stomach. The baby!

She screamed. But it was short-lived. He was on top of her now, one hand bearing down on her throat, cutting off her air supply. She had both hands clutched around his other wrist, pushing to keep that ring and its poisonous bite from touching her.

But she was growing weak. She needed air. The ring came down like the grasping hands from her nightmare. A pounding rhythm filled up her ears. No. Her baby. Her baby! They had to live. Rafe needed them both to live.

Summoning the last of her waning strength, she tried to kick, but she was too weak to do more than squirm beneath him. Her vision went murky. Her elbows started to bend. She was going to die. She was—

A thunderous sound roared through the tent as a big black, tank-like van tore through the walls, sent tables and chairs flying and crashed into the ice machine. A broken table hit her attacker in the back, knocking him down and loosening his grip.

The sudden influx of oxygen into her lungs cleared her head and restored her sight. She saw figures in black swarming out of the van like hornets from the hive.

"Get on the ground, now!"

"Josie!"

She shoved at Beecher's chest. She tried to tell them about Randy, to warn them about the ring. But her voice made no sound in her bruised throat.

"Gun!"

"Gun!"

The weight on her eased, for only a moment. And then Jeffrey Beecher rolled to his feet, wrapping his arm around Josie's neck and grinding the barrel of Randy's Glock into her temple. "Get back! All of you, get back or I shoot her right now!"

"Sarge!"

Captain Cutler's warning went unheeded.

Rafe took one step toward her, then two, three, four, five, his gun locked between his hands and aimed at the middle of Jeffrey Beecher's forehead.

"Get back!" Beecher ordered, pushing his gun so hard against her skull that her head tilted to the left.

Whiskey-brown eyes locked on to hers, full of love,

full of anger, full of something of such deadly intent that even Josie trembled.

"Is this the Rich Girl Killer?" Rafe demanded in a low, gravelly voice.

"Yes," she answered.

"Put down your damn guns!"

But Rafael Delgado's eyes never wavered. "Captain, I have a shot."

"Take it."

He pulled the trigger.

Jeffrey Beecher jerked.

Warm blood that was not her own spattered her cheek.

And when Beecher's collapsing body would have dragged her down to the ground with him, she never even touched the grass.

Rafe was there to catch her in his arms.

He turned to carry her to the back of the SWAT van. And while she clung to his neck, too stunned to even weep, she saw Alex Taylor and Trip Jones stowing their guns as they knelt over Beecher's body to look for a pulse they would never find.

"Poison. His ring…" she rasped through her raw throat. "Careful."

Without breaking stride, Rafe relayed the information to his team and sat with her in his lap.

She saw Miranda Murdock, her head bleeding, her clothes dirty, stumble into the tent and hand her rifle over to Michael Cutler. She was so weak she could barely stand on her own. "Is Josie okay?"

"She will be," the captain answered, sitting Randy in a chair and checking her injuries. "We all will be."

Josie nodded against Rafe's solid chest and let her eyes drift shut. These people were her friends. They were her family.

She wasn't alone.

"SERGEANT, IF WE could get a listen to the baby's heartbeat again."

"You said the baby was fine."

"Yes, but we want to make sure there are no sudden drops in pressure. They'll be doing the same thing when we get her to the hospital. So if we could just…?"

Rafe was making it difficult for the paramedics on the scene to conduct their examination of Josie, but he didn't want to let her go. And he sure as hell didn't want to share this time with Spencer Montgomery sticking his nose in at every turn to ask another question.

"The poison ring should give us a chemical matchup to Austin's murder." The detective scratched some more notes on his pad. "And Nick's already at Beecher's house. He's found a room full of trophies from each of his murders. An earring from Gretchen Cosgrove, a baby blanket he took from Valeska Gallagher—plus countless files and news clippings on Audrey Kline and Charlotte Mayweather. We believe he still intended to murder them once you were eliminated and he couldn't be identified."

Josie turned on the ambulance gurney to face the red-haired detective. "So you finally got your man."

He tucked his notebook inside the pocket of his suit jacket and nodded. "Thanks to you. Not many people would have come forward once they realized who and what they'd seen. You're a brave woman, Josie Nichols."

"My father would have expected nothing less." Rafe welcomed the squeeze on his hand. "Of either of us."

Detective Montgomery reluctantly included Rafe in his thanks. "You robbed me of my chance to interrogate the suspect, Sergeant."

"I wasn't going to let him hurt her."

"Why do you think I let her have her way about the safe house?" Spencer held out his hand. "I'd have done the same thing if Beecher had threatened someone I loved."

Rafe took his hand. "I still don't like you."

"I don't like you, either." He saluted Josie before turning away. "Invite me to the wedding."

"Wedding?" Josie echoed, her throat raw from Beecher's hands there.

"He's getting ahead of himself. Enough." Rafe pushed the paramedic away for a few private moments. He'd washed the RGK's blood off Josie's skin himself. But there was still spatter in her hair. He hated that he'd done that, that he'd had to use his deadly skill with Josie so close at hand. He cupped her face between his palms and kissed her. Her lips parted and answered, and emotions too powerful to deny any longer rushed up and made him dizzy. Finally, he pulled his mouth away and cupped his hand over her belly. The danger had come far too close to the baby, too. "How's Junior?"

Her hands folded over his. "What if Junior turns out to be a girl? We'll have to come up with a new nickname."

He wished he had some witty, romantic comeback. But he was the man he was, and words had never been a gift. "How about Delgado? I want to marry you. I want to be a daddy to this baby." He touched his forehead to hers and his heart spilled out. "I want… Oh, God, Jose… I love you so much. I love this baby. I was so scared I was going to lose you and I was never going to get the chance to tell you that I finally wised up and believed what you knew all along."

She lifted one hand to stroke his jaw with her soothing touch. "That we were meant to be together?"

"That I *can* love—that I *do* love. You." He turned his face to press a kiss into her palm. "Hell, honey, I've got nothing without you. I *am* nothing without you."

"Don't say that. You are the best man I know. I've always known that you're a real hero—that you're my hero. Don't ever say that you're nothing."

He nodded, maybe halfway believing her for the first time. "I've been a miserable man for a long time, Jose. I've been afraid of giving a damn about anyone. Be with me. Help me to not be afraid anymore. Let me love you."

"And the baby?"

"I can take classes. I can learn from the example Aaron set. I can learn to be a good dad."

She pressed her palm over his heart. "You already know how, Rafe. You've got it all in here. Just love us."

"I can do that." He kissed her to let her know how much he did love her. And then, just because he wanted to, he kissed her again. "So, are you going to marry me?"

"Yes."

He held his woman and his child, their child, in his arms. "What do you think your father would say?"

"That it's about damn time."

Epilogue

Three months later

"Oh, no you don't." Miranda Murdock was practically frantic as she popped up out of her patio chair in Michael Cutler's backyard and held up her hands to push away the tiny bundle. "I can't."

Jillian Cutler, the captain's young wife, laughed. "It's a baby, Randy. He won't bite."

Ready to give birth in about a month herself, the tall brunette seemed especially attached to the role of newborn babysitter.

"Exactly," Randy protested. "I'm all for other women having kids, but it's just not my thing. And this one is so, so little."

Rafe swooped in from the male contingent of guests who'd been opening a beer while the captain grilled steaks and burgers and brats for the party. He took the tiny bundle of perfection from Jillian's arms and rubbed noses with his son, Aaron Robert Delgado. "He's only three days old, Murdock. Give him a few years to grow before you start flirtin' with him."

"How's my sweetheart?" Rafe caught his breath as Josie came out the deck's French doors with a tray of food she was carrying for her Uncle Robbie, who limped out with his cane behind her. His heart swelled, as it did each time he realized that Josie was his wife, that she loved him and that she'd given him every reason to believe in happily-ever-afters.

He leaned down and kissed her. "You talkin' to me or the baby?"

She smiled that gorgeous smile. "Both."

"Have I congratulated you on your graduation from nursing school today, Mrs. Delgado?"

She went all maternal on him and pulled little Aaron's hat more squarely over his head to protect his delicate skin from the August sun. But when she smiled up at him, Rafe's pulse raced. Now *that* look was definitely not maternal. Oh, man, how was he going to wait six weeks for her to be able to make love again?

"I thought this was my celebration," she teased, as always reading his hopes and needs in that caring, humbling, perceptive way of hers. She dropped her voice to a whisper and made his blood bubble with impatience. "But I'm counting the days, too."

"All right. Gather round," Captain Cutler announced, dropping his arm around his wife's shoulders and kissing her cheek before he spoke to the group. "Before we eat, I have an announcement to make."

Alex and Trip made the appropriate groans and razzing noises. Both were appropriately quieted by their wives. Audrey Kline and Alex Taylor's wedding had been the social event of the summer, with coverage in all the papers. They lived in a downtown loft and she was a force to be reckoned with in the district attorney's office. Yet despite all that money and class, she was as down to earth as Alex—and as loyal and loving a partner as any cop deserved.

Charlotte Jones seemed to be coming out of her shell more and more, especially now that the man who'd tried to kill her earlier in the year was dead. Rafe didn't know the bespectacled archaeologist all that well yet. But she made Trip happy. The big guy turned into a marshmallow whenever she called, and his sudden passion for old things and camping trips left Rafe thinking the two shared a lot more than their love of books when he took a leave to go on one of her research jaunts.

"So what's your announcement, Captain?" Trip asked, coming up behind Charlotte to hold her hand.

The captain patted his wife's belly. "I'm going to be taking a six-week paternity leave soon. And I just wanted to let you know that while I'm out of the office, you're going to have a new boss."

"Who's that?" Alex asked.

Captain Cutler turned to look at Rafe. "You're ready for it, Sarge. You want the job of running SWAT Team One?"

Rafe was overwhelmed. He'd had three father figures in his life. One was a nightmare. The other was dead. And one was this man whom he respected highly, the man who'd given him a lot of leeway when he'd needed to protect Josie, and when it had come time to take out the Rich Girl Killer.

This man believed in him.

He had well and truly outgrown the influence of his parents and his tortured childhood. He was ready for this.

Josie nudged him with her elbow. "Say something."

Right. Words. Not his best thing. "Okay."

"Okay?"

Alex tapped him on the shoulder. "Congratulations, Sarge."

"Inspiring speech," Trip teased.

Randy came up to shake his hand, carefully avoiding contact with little Aaron. "Are you going to let me shoot the bad guy next time? I am the sharpshooter on this team."

"I'm coming back," the captain reminded them.

"Good. Take the time you need, Captain. But I'm expecting you to return." Rafe's gaze included his wife, his son and all his friends here. "I like it when my family's all together."

* * * * *

Watch for the next
THE PRECINCT: SWAT *story, NANNY 911,*
featuring sharpshooter Miranda Murdock.

Harlequin®

INTRIGUE®

COMING NEXT MONTH

Available September 13, 2011

> You can find more information on upcoming Harlequin® titles, free excerpts and more at
> **www.HarlequinInsideRomance.com.**

HICNM0811

REQUEST YOUR FREE BOOKS!
2 FREE NOVELS PLUS 2 FREE GIFTS!

◆ Harlequin®

INTRIGUE®

BREATHTAKING ROMANTIC SUSPENSE

YES! Please send me 2 FREE Harlequin Intrigue® novels and my 2 FREE gifts (gifts are worth about $10). After receiving them, if I don't wish to receive any more books, I can return the shipping statement marked "cancel." If I don't cancel, I will receive 6 brand-new novels every month and be billed just $4.49 per book in the U.S. or $5.24 per book in Canada. That's a saving of at least 14% off the cover price! It's quite a bargain! Shipping and handling is just 50¢ per book in the U.S. and 75¢ per book in Canada.* I understand that accepting the 2 free books and gifts places me under no obligation to buy anything. I can always return a shipment and cancel at any time. Even if I never buy another book, the two free books and gifts are mine to keep forever.

182/382 HDN FEQ2

Name _____ (PLEASE PRINT)

Address _____ Apt. #

City _____ State/Prov. _____ Zip/Postal Code

Signature (if under 18, a parent or guardian must sign)

Mail to the **Reader Service:**
IN U.S.A.: P.O. Box 1867, Buffalo, NY 14240-1867
IN CANADA: P.O. Box 609, Fort Erie, Ontario L2A 5X3

Not valid for current subscribers to Harlequin Intrigue books.

**Are you a subscriber to Harlequin Intrigue books
and want to receive the larger-print edition?
Call 1-800-873-8635 or visit www.ReaderService.com.**

* Terms and prices subject to change without notice. Prices do not include applicable taxes. Sales tax applicable in N.Y. Canadian residents will be charged applicable taxes. Offer not valid in Quebec. This offer is limited to one order per household. All orders subject to credit approval. Credit or debit balances in a customer's account(s) may be offset by any other outstanding balance owed by or to the customer. Please allow 4 to 6 weeks for delivery. Offer available while quantities last.

Your Privacy—The Reader Service is committed to protecting your privacy. Our Privacy Policy is available online at www.ReaderService.com or upon request from the Reader Service.

We make a portion of our mailing list available to reputable third parties that offer products we believe may interest you. If you prefer that we not exchange your name with third parties, or if you wish to clarify or modify your communication preferences, please visit us at www.ReaderService.com/consumerschoice or write to us at Reader Service Preference Service, P.O. Box 9062, Buffalo, NY 14269. Include your complete name and address.

HI11B

New York Times *and* USA TODAY *bestselling author*
Maya Banks presents a brand-new miniseries

PREGNANCY & PASSION

When four irresistible tycoons face
the consequences of temptation.

Book 1—*ENTICED BY HIS FORGOTTEN LOVER*

Available September 2011 from Harlequin® Desire®!

Rafael de Luca had been in bad situations before. A crowded ballroom could never make him sweat.

These people would never know that he had no memory of any of them.

He surveyed the party with grim tolerance, searching for the source of his unease.

At first his gaze flickered past her, but he yanked his attention back to a woman across the room. Her stare bored holes through him. Unflinching and steady, even when his eyes locked with hers.

Petite, even in heels, she had a creamy olive complexion. A wealth of inky-black curls cascaded over her shoulders and her eyes were equally dark.

She looked at him as if she'd already judged him and found him lacking. He'd never seen her before in his life. Or had he?

He cursed the gaping hole in his memory. He'd been diagnosed with selective amnesia after his accident four months ago. Which seemed like complete and utter bull. No one got amnesia except hysterical women in bad soap operas.

With a smile, he disengaged himself from the group

around him and made his way to the mystery woman.

She wasn't coy. She stared straight at him as he approached, her chin thrust upward in defiance.

"Excuse me, but have we met?" he asked in his smoothest voice.

His gaze moved over the generous swell of her breasts pushed up by the empire waist of her black cocktail dress.

When he glanced back up at her face, he saw fury in her eyes.

"Have we *met?*" Her voice was barely a whisper, but he felt each word like the crack of a whip.

Before he could process her response, she nailed him with a right hook. He stumbled back, holding his nose.

One of his guards stepped between Rafe and the woman, accidentally sending her to one knee. Her hand flew to the folds of her dress.

It was then, as she cupped her belly, that the realization hit him. She was pregnant.

Her eyes flashing, she turned and ran down the marble hallway.

Rafael ran after her. He burst from the hotel lobby, and saw two shoes sparkling in the moonlight, twinkling at him.

He blew out his breath in frustration and then shoved the pair of sparkly, ultrafeminine heels at his head of security.

"Find the woman who wore these shoes."

Will Rafael find his mystery woman?
Find out in Maya Banks's passionate new novel
ENTICED BY HIS FORGOTTEN LOVER
Available September 2011 from Harlequin® Desire®!

Love and family secrets collide in
a powerful new trilogy from

Linda Warren

the Hardin Boys

Blood is thicker than oil

Coming August 9, 2011.

The Texan's Secret

Before Chance Hardin can join his brothers in
their new oil business, he must reveal a secret
that could tear their family apart. And his
desire for family has never been stronger, all
because of beautiful Shay Dumont.
A woman with a secret of her own....

The Texan's Bride
(October 11, 2011)

The Texan's Christmas
(December 6, 2011)